Praise for

"A book full of desire, lies, and deceit, *Beautiful Lies* is this year's must read."

—Lady Amber's Reviews

"This book is compelling and one that cannot be missed! The story captures you from the start, and it's impossible to put down. I would definitely read this book multiple times and can't wait to read more from Gina Whitney!"

—This Redhead Loves Books

"*Beautiful Lies* was a roller-coaster ride from beginning to end. The story felt like a cross between *The Devil's Advocate* and *Romeo and Juliet* with a sexy twist. If you love stories with a little angst, a lot of drama, and smoking passion then this is a story you will enjoy!"

—The BookChick BlogReviews

Beautiful Lies

Gina Whitney

Follow Gina Whitney on Twitter @ginamwhitney and on Facebook.

Book design by:
Arbor Books, Inc.
www.arborbooks.com

Printed in the United States of America.

Beautiful Lies
Gina Whitney

1. Title   2. Author   3. Erotic Romance

Library of Congress Control Number: 2014905479
ISBN 13: 978-0-615-99157-3

Dedication

I'd like to thank my boyfriend, lover, and best friend, Rafael. Writers oftentimes go off into their own worlds. I seem to live in mine. Having a partner who accepts this fact is vital for our relationship's survival. Luckily, I have the best boyfriend, who loves me unconditionally and supports me in everything I do. Rafael, you're the most amazing person, and I do not deserve you. I adore you. You own my heart.

Acknowledgments

My boys, PJ and Drew, my funny, passionate, brilliant, raging hormonal teenage sons, as well as my boyfriend's children, Gianna and RJ, you have been super supportive, encouraging, excited, and understanding with my writing. Thank you for being the best children a mom could ever hope for. I love you more than you know.

To the amazing bloggers and authors who have shared, pimped, and beta read, you all work tirelessly mostly behind the scenes to read, review, pimp, and get readers to one-click and share. I oftentimes think you never get the proper thanks for all you do. Kudos and love to you and all you do daily. You do what you love and love what you do, and that doesn't go unnoticed by me. I love you all, and if I could wrap you up in a giant hug, I would. BookChickBlogReviews, I love my mocha chick something fierce. Christine Stanley and Kristen Karwen, you're my sisters from another mister for sure. I'm so very glad we met and became friends.

To my beta readers: Thank you. Thank you. Thank you. Your support and input has made this book what it is. I feel fortunate to have found you. Love you all!

To my One-Click Chicks, who tirelessly pimp, share, and blog with smiles on your faces and love in your hearts, which truly humbles me. If I could take you on a tropical vacation (girls only) to thank you all properly, I would.

To my PA Lady Ambers Reviews, aka Amber Garcia, aka my chick, aka A, aka my biatch, I am so very thankful that the stars aligned on the day I met you. I cannot express fully my deepest appreciation for you and what your loyalty, support, and friendship mean to me. I will forever be your friend, support you, love you, and be loyal. Your hella hot teasers, banners, and attention to detail are ridiculous. Not to mention the epic weekend we had in New York City or the fact that I can't listen to Katy Perry's "Dark Horse" or Beyonce's "Drunk in Love" without LMAO and thinking of you. We make an epic team. Thank you for always having my back, chick!

Regina from May I Designs, thank you, doll. Love my trailer, and thank you for bringing my vision to fruition. You are one talented, kickass chick that I'm looking forward to continuing working with.

To my readers, thank you all. I'm still blown away by your tweets, posts, PMs, reviews, support, and emails. I can't express to you what it means to be a proud indie author. I never believed for one day that I would achieve a tenth of what has gone on this year. I still have quite a way to go. To say I'm humbled by you wouldn't adequately describe the depth of gratitude I have. You've helped me realize a dream as a writer. Having you pick up one of my books, enjoy the story, love the characters, and want more leaves me with love in my heart and a smile on my face. I am grateful. Hopefully, you are able to escape for a few hours or days, leaving you feeling the same way ;). You rock!

To my cheerleaders: Aunt Sue, who attends seven o'clock mass every morning and listens tentatively to all my sex talk and cursing, and who is always encouraging and supportive; Alice, who cheers me any time day or night (and who's become obsessed with smut); and my sister, who always has a way of keeping me grounded and laughing.

Thanks to Lauren Berju Stanco for helping me find the perfect quote for *Beautiful Lies*.

Joel, Terri, Elise, Olga, and Jessica, thank you for all your incredible work and for tolerating my obscene mouth and thoughts. I truly appreciate everything.

"I prefer to be broken with the ugly truth rather than fall in love with your beautiful lies."
Unknown

Chapter One

If I had known then that Lilly Amsel would set such a fierce blaze in my life, I would have taken the next elevator.

All I wanted that morning was to get a hard run on the treadmill and go to my office to put in some weekend overtime. I arrived at The Equity, the most prestigious gym not only in New York City but in the country, and was checking my work-issued Blackberry as usual. I tended to avoid such pretentious settings, but membership was one of the many perks of my employment at Wotherspoon and Associates. As a law student at Aldensburg University, I had interned at the corporate law firm and had been offered a position after I'd passed the bar five years ago. Aldensburg was not as premier a college when compared to the Ivies; in fact most people have never heard of it. But, like me, it got the job done. And professionally the job I was trying to get done now was making partner. I know it was an ambitious goal, but I had nothing but faith in my skills to make it happen.

For the moment I was there at The Equity in my sagging basketball shorts and stretched-out T-shirt, standing amid chichi air kissers. I was not there to hobnob; I actually had a serious goal. I worked out not only to maintain my body but to keep my mind sharp, focused, and ready at all times. That was what separated me from those people. I was a shark among peacocks.

The cheerless receptionist with the sucked-in cheeks eyed me as I stepped through the door. I could see her hostile nostrils widen like a bull's as she feigned a barely polite smile. She knew who I was but played this ridiculous game with me every day. Always pretending not to know me. "I'm sorry, sir. You must be looking for the gym down the street."

That was her way of telling me that my choice of clothing was not up to par, and I might consider some more appropriate attire. I had known plenty of people like her growing up and knew that the best way to handle her was to be in her face every chance I got, to be the proverbial pebble in her shoe. I swiped my security pass card and told her, "See you tomorrow."

The Equity was an "it" destination for celebrities and all manner of the rich and powerful. The entry level consisted of a wide, stark-white hallway with electric-blue tube lights lining the walls and ceiling, and filled with the ethereal melody of a string orchestra. This main hallway connected with several more, the last one ending in a spacious, low-lit lounge area. Scattered about were suede couches and glass tables; black-and-white photos of perfectly sculpted body parts hung on the walls. This was where those who came to be seen strategically posed themselves just in case an undercover paparazzo managed to sneak in. The lounge was usually empty in the morning because its denizens could not manage to roll out of bed until well into the afternoon.

I made my way across the rugs to yet another hall that led to a bank of elevators. I pushed the "up" button, eager to start my workout. Then I heard the quick click clack of feminine footsteps come up behind me. I sighed because I knew those shoes—probably high heels—were not made for running. This was just another pampered pest whose idea of working out was getting a massage. I did not even have to turn around to figure this chick out.

Her heavy perfume was layered with the fresh smell of soap and shampoo. Typical of someone who saw the gym as a social occasion rather than a place to exercise. I never had patience with lackadaisical people who were not willing to put in the effort to achieve anything. I wanted so badly to turn around and say, "Why are you even here? Shouldn't you be having Sunday brunch over at Peacock Alley?"

However, I was not there to judge. I was there to work out. But I was curious as to who was standing behind me. I looked into the stainless-steel door of the elevator to see if I could make out the reflection. The dull surface only revealed that the grayish silhouette behind me was tall and lanky. Not as tall as me at six foot three but tall nonetheless.

Then a hoard of more click-clacking footsteps arrived, accompanied by raucously shrill voices greeting the first woman. I thought, *Oh, God. Jersey girls.*

"Lilly!" they all screamed in unison.

The first woman, Lilly, chirped back, "Sweetie pies, how are you?"

One nasal voice responded, "Fine if you like your nipples turning into Popsicles. It's cold as hell out there. What's on your agenda today?"

"Pilates with Jean-Paul. Thirty minutes."

"What is he? A slave driver?" another woman said seriously with a croaky smoker's voice.

"I know, right?" Lilly agreed. All I could do was roll my eyes at that nonsense.

Lilly had an odd way of speaking that only a discerning ear

could pick up. She was trying her best to affect a newscaster accent, that plain Midwestern way of speaking. However, she would occasionally slip into an upward inflection that made every sentence sound like a question. She was definitely a SoCal transplant. It was beyond me why, in the midst of shudder-inducing Jersey accents, Lilly hid her natural one.

As the elevator numbers slowly ticked down, I noticed in my peripheral vision the number of men passing. They were all doing double takes at Lilly. Either she was gorgeous or hideous beyond measure. Either way, it did not matter to me. I had seen plenty of both and was not swayed by the slop or gloss of anything. An ethics professor a long way back even accused me of being jaded. What he could not understand was that when your life has been a trial by fire, you see things differently from most. The world and all the people in it are just opportunities for you to get what you need. You can't depend on anyone but yourself. When you have lived in a cushioned bubble like the professor, you just don't get that. Needless to say I barely passed that class.

The elevator finally arrived, and the herd of new-money cows stampeded past me to get in. I turned back, and Lilly was waiting for me to usher her in like I was the doorman. Sure enough she was decked out in black from head to toe—leggings, turtleneck, and those clacking ankle boots. She had on so much black that she looked like she was imitating midnight. To top it all off, she had a leather bag brimming with Voss water and vitamin blister packs.

Lilly appeared to be in her early twenties, so I was perplexed as to why she needed so many pills. Still, I must admit that I was taken aback by how beautiful she was. Her hair, pushed back and glossed into a tight bun, reminded me of dark honey, and her graceful, lithe body looked like that of a ballet dancer. And those eyes—they were extraordinarily large orbs of malachite rimmed in chestnut. However, no matter how pouty her dewy lips were, Lilly still acted like an entitled elitist, so pampered that she probably considered Park Slope to be the ghetto.

I watched her standing there looking at me. This woman was used to people fawning all over her, and I was not one to do that. I did not grovel or bow down to anybody. But no matter what I felt about her at the moment, I decided to do the gentlemanly thing.

"Ladies first," I said.

Lilly sashayed past me and joined her tacky and deeply moneyed crew. As she crossed the threshold of the elevator, she gave me a "thanks" that was nowhere near sincere. I spent the elevator ride to the third floor listening to her companions' boisterous gossip about other women at the club. Yet I did not hear Lilly utter any comment. I just felt her eyes laser beaming my back. Apparently she was still shocked and pissed that I didn't think she was the shit.

"Lilly, you forgot your water," Jean-Paul yelled out to me. He had been my Pilates instructor for the past six years—my entire time in New York. After I finished my thirty-minute workout with him, I got some fresh acrylics in the spa. I was preparing for an interview with *Paramour Life*, fashion's most prominent magazine, later that afternoon. Though I was modeling, the interview was not about me. It was really about my boyfriend of two years, Sig Krok. Sig had come from Sweden twenty years ago and started his own fashion house, Klå. Klå. It quickly became one of the best-selling clothing lines in the world. This article would be a tribute to Sig. The magazine just wanted my perspective on him and a little insider knowledge of our highly visible yet terribly private relationship.

With discreet sleight of hand, Jean-Paul handed me my property, and it was not really water. It was my bottle of Klonopin.

"I know how important *water* is," he said then quickly dismissed himself to his next scheduled client. I watched him for a moment. I was in awe and bewilderment over how he mastered the art of prancing and swaying like a seasoned burlesque dancer. He really had to teach me that sometime.

Realizing I was running out of time before the interview and still had to get my makeup done, I abruptly turned around to leave. And I turned right into Mr. Scowl—the guy at the elevator this morning. *Aw, just great*, I thought.

"Excuse me," I said as I started walking away. By then he had put on some more weather-appropriate clothing—jeans and a discount sweater with a white T-shirt underneath. And the creep did not even respond to me, smirking his arrogant mouth instead. Even though he was pompous, he was kind of cute. Though it was the middle of winter, his skin looked sun kissed. He was a giant of a man, well over six feet tall. His luminous, copper eyes seemed like they were always narrowed, like he was annoyed with people because they were merely human and could not withstand his survey.

I headed toward the elevator, and he did the same. When we got there, I started pushing buttons in hopes it would make the elevator come faster. The bell dinged, and he let me on first. I could tell he didn't want to but was trying to be The Man. We stood in opposite corners. By then most men would have engaged me in conversation. He hadn't. Was he gay? No, I had a fairly accurate gaydar. What was wrong with him then? I was becoming increasingly irritated by this man's presence. I glanced over at him. He was wiping his sweaty brow, and his hand pushed up his cap a bit, exposing his inky hair cut with perfect precision around the edges. The cap was thready and had a large A on the front. He probably had gotten it from some college a while back. I also noticed that on the underside of the cap's bill, he had written his name in permanent marker: Cam.

Even though he grated on me, I could not help but be distracted by his body. He had Adonis-like shoulders, broad and protective. His thick thighs were agape, his wide stance taking up a good deal of space. This square-jawed man was definitely broody, but even without a smile, I could make out the dimple in his cheek. And I did not even want to get started on the size of his hands and feet. They were *enormous*.

The air vent was blowing a light, steady stream of air across Cam. I inhaled the heady scent of his newly sweaty body intermingled with a woodsy deodorant. I leaned in his direction. One of my eyes went on autopilot and fluttered—that thing that happens when something is really good. I took another breath and leaned in some more.

Wait! What...the fuck...am I doing? I caught myself right before my nose landed on Cam's arm. And there he was with the same "what the fuck?" look. He was staring at me going for his pit with my crazy eye. He obviously thought I was about to rape him.

Quick, deflect. I pointed at my ear. "I thought you said something." I regained my composure and returned my gaze forward.

But he sure did smell good. And, boy, was I horny.

Whatever. I wasn't going to say anything else to Cam. He was still nothing but an aloof, smug asshole to me. And I had to endure what seemed like a forever ride to the first floor with him. I turned my face back to the elevator doors with just the sound of the motors and cables to break the silence.

I was so relieved to get out of the elevator, I practically sprinted into the parking garage. I slung my faux fur over my shoulders as I rushed to Sig's Infiniti QX80. Cam was trailing me, sliding into his leather jacket. And I just knew he was about to ask me for my number despite that fiasco in the elevator. Maybe I hadn't lost my touch. I was prepared to shoot him down, of course. But he sure was taking his time. I was already at Sig's SUV.

However, not only did Cam *not* ask me for my number, he was only walking behind me because he had parked his powerful, black Harley 1200 Custom next to me. He spread his thick legs and straddled it then put on his Aviator sunglasses and revved up his baby. I had to say, that motorcycle…the way it just hung between his legs…looked more like a big, hard dick than anything else.

Cam turned the twistgrip like it was his cock and throttled up. The rumble from the motorcycle bounced off the concrete walls of the garage. It was almost deafening. He didn't care. In fact, if I hadn't known any better, I would have sworn he'd done it on purpose. I was totally conflicted. Never had I so detested a man and still wanted to fuck the skin off his dick at the same time.

Alas, Cam drove off without even looking in my direction. I let out an audible gasp. No straight male ever looked at me and just turned away.

Hmm...maybe my gaydar was in need of a tune-up.

Chapter Two

"Miss Lilly, which do you prefer?" the makeup artist asked me.

I did not know the artist's name. She was just one of many Sig had hired to make me look appropriate enough to fit his image. I picked out a brilliant shade of turquoise shadow to go on my eyes. As I watched myself in the Hollywood mirror, I could see the reflection of Sig's self-portrait behind me. That awful oil painting always gave me the willies. It was of monstrous proportions and loomed over the entire room. And it was true to life. Sig looked like an anthropological forty-five-degree angle. Everything about him was square, sharp, and pointy. There was absolutely no softness about him. The way his white-blond hair blended seamlessly into his almost transparent skin and nearly colorless eyes was disconcerting at best.

What Sig lacked in warmth and humanity, he made up for in ego, and he wanted to document his life for posterity. I was an extension of that mythical life like furniture was to a house. That is why he had me shadowed a few days a week by Tamara, his personal photographer. Tamara grew up in Trinidad and was a bouncing ball of sunshine. She was a proud Trini woman, gorgeous enough to be a model herself. Every visit with her was like a relaxing trip to the tropics, which I needed after being under Sig's constant scrutiny. Over the past few weeks,

Tamara had become a confidante of sorts. Of course I did not tell her *everything*. When the cosmetologist left, Tamara started snapping photos of me. "Girly," she said, "aren't you a busy woman? Today the interview. Tomorrow the big gala. You're going to be totally worn down."

I stood at the mirror and adjusted my demi bra. "Yes, but this is the life of a famous man's girlfriend."

Tamara looked through my custom-built closet that was the size of two bedrooms. It was overflowing with designer clothing, footwear, and jewels. She put her hand on her hip and said, "It looks like you're really suffering. What's up with the spokesperson position for Klå? Do you still want it?"

"Are you kidding? A chance to be the face of Klå? Be what Brooke Shields was for Calvin Klein? That is the biggest modeling gig ever. I'd never have to do another catalog again."

"You'd think because you're his girlfriend, Sig would just give it to you."

"Sig doesn't operate like that. Business is business. Home is home. My function right now is to be an asset for his image." I looked back at the mirror. "And I am getting older."

Tamara stood right in front of me and took a direct photo of my face. She asked, "Do you love him?"

I had already asked myself that question a million times and always came back with the same answer. Sig was like a fog machine. As he spewed mist, I was able to hide behind the haze of his life. Sig, like modeling, validated my existence. Lord knows I couldn't. All I had to do was keep the real me—the me that was damaged beyond repair—tucked away in some recess. Essentially I was nothing more than a fraud.

So when Tamara asked me about true love, I could only go off my experience. And experience taught me that everyone is fucked up. True love has to do with authenticity, and everyone is living a lie. How can love happen in a sea of illusion?

"I have been with him for years. Of course I have developed affection for him," I answered honestly.

I was thankful to hear the doorbell ring so I would not have to continue that conversation. "The reporter is here," I said, adjusting my wrap dress.

As I went to the door, Tamara stopped me as she pushed one of her many locks behind her ear. "Lilly, you still haven't answered my question."

"Yes, I did."

"No, you didn't. Do you love Sig?"

I turned her question around: "Can anyone let themselves be real enough to truly love and be loved by another?"

———

I just couldn't figure out why I had no emotional connection with Rebecca.

Rebecca was a tiny thing, highly intelligent, with a degree in biochemistry. She was an interesting conversationalist and made me laugh occasionally. She was waiting tables to pay her way through grad school. That's how I met her—during one of those times when that weird, lonely feeling crept up on me. But something was missing…something fundamental, basic.

And here we were again on another Sunday night, fucking. It was almost like it was on my to-do list: pay the bills, do laundry, fuck Rebecca.

Rebecca was on top of me bouncing up and down. She must have read somewhere that men like watching skin flicks, and she was doing a bad imitation of a porn star. I tried not to laugh as she threw her head back, ran her fingers through her pixie cut, and moaned like she had just gotten shot in the stomach.

"Cam! Cam! Cam!" she grunted and yelled. Goddamn it. I was two seconds away from stuffing my dirty sock in her mouth to make her shut the hell up.

It didn't matter how loud Rebecca screamed, though. She could make as much noise as she wanted because I was the only occupant in the building. Ever since I was a teen, I learned how to save and invest my money. I had to. By the time I finished law school, my investments had paid off, and I was able to purchase this distressed warehouse building cheap, which was surprising in New York. I did all the rehab myself. The first level still basically looked like an industrialized space. However, on the second level, I created a series of lofts. I had the largest one. My intention was to one day rent out the rest, but for now I just wanted to be by myself. In the end, with all the refurbishing, I wound up with a pretty nifty property that is coveted by developers.

I heard Rebecca's stuttered groans. She was cumming. I always held out until a woman climaxed; I was never going to be that premature-ejaculating dude. But since Rebecca got hers, it was okay for me to get mine, and I did. Though the sex was intense at times, it was not the height of physical ecstasy and was emotionally stunted. I figured I was overthinking the situation with Rebecca and needed to be satisfied with the way things were. It was safer that way. To never care if she disappeared like everyone else in my life had done.

I rolled over on my back. The night was essentially over for me. I was trying to think of a new way to tell her to leave without actually saying it. I did want to be polite, you know. But Rebecca was stalling. She started studying a framed photograph of the mountain cabin I had recently purchased in Upstate New York. It was a small cabin but had sweeping views of the Catskill Mountains. It even had a small pond and stream out back.

"God, Cam, you've had this cabin for months now. When are you going to take me to see it?"

I thought, *Never.* But I replied, "We'll see, Rebecca."

"I told you to call me Becky. 'Rebecca' sounds so formal. Everyone close to me calls me Becky."

I did not consider myself to be close to Rebecca, but she was putting the pressure on me to commit. She tried to lie on my chest; however, I managed to block her by putting my hand over my heart. I thought she would have picked up on that not-so-subtle hint, but she was on a mission.

"How about I stay over tonight? I mean we've been dating for a year—"

"Well, not exactly dating."

"Yeah, dating. I think it's about time I spent the night. I mean are you hiding something from me?"

I did not want to go through this again. "I have work in the morning. A ton of files. I really need to rest up. Maybe some other time."

Rebecca was miffed at me but was not about to cause a commotion. She was playing it smart by making sure she did not do anything to jeopardize her chances of becoming my official girlfriend and more.

"Okay, silly goose, some other time," she said with a grin.

"But you know women like me can be easily snatched up by the competition."

I stifled a laugh at that veiled threat. If I had any competition, she would have been gone by now. "I hear you."

"I'm serious, Cam. I'm not going to say it twice."

"Then don't."

With a huff, Rebecca bounded out of bed and rounded up her clothing that was scattered about the room. I watched her eye my ratty college T-shirt and worn-out sweatpants. She coveted my clothing. She wanted to have the exclusive privilege of wearing it like a real girlfriend.

After Rebecca got dressed, I wrapped my waist in a sheet and walked her to the door. She spread her arms wide to engulf me. I patted her back and opened the door. She deflated and said, "Same time next Sunday?"

"We'll see."

I stayed there to make sure Rebecca got on the elevator. Then I went to my window to watch her get into the car. I did not do this because I cared about her safety. I was simply making sure she was gone.

My belly started talking to me, and I realized that I had not eaten all day. I went to the fridge and luckily had some leftover lasagna bolognese and antipasto. I ate this combination way too frequently, but these two recipes were the only ones I could remember my mother cooking for me before she died. She was an Italian immigrant from a well-to-do family. She enjoyed a good life until she met my father, a hard-living, uneducated WASP…and my childhood demon.

I sat down in my favorite leather chair, nice and cracked, and started to eat my post-coitus meal. An unopened envelope with a return address belonging to Hilda Brown sat on the coffee table. She was my next-door neighbor when I was a little boy. The last time I heard from her was fifteen years ago. I had been procrastinating about opening the letter. I knew what it was. If I was going to open that envelope, I knew I had better do it right then. If I did not, I would have tossed it in the trash. I took a bite of pepperoni as if it would prepare me somehow and opened the envelope. Sure enough it was what I thought it was: an invitation to a memorial service for my deceased mother.

I tossed the invitation back on the table and looked out the window at the hazy, setting sun. I noted how awesome it looked. If it were possible, it would be a perfect place to escape to at that moment. My thoughts began to drift, and a surprising remembrance of Lilly crossed my mind. I blew it off and turned on the TV instead. As I watched a boxing match, more intrusive thoughts about Lilly kept popping into my head.

Chapter Three

Unlike most people, I loved Monday mornings. The weekends always seemed like a waste of time, doing nonsensical things of no real value. That is why I spent as much time as I could down at Wotherspoon and Associates. I was driven to be productive, and stress, competition, and adrenaline were my fuels. What would I achieve by the day's end? Which crisis would my firm come to me to avert? I could not wait to get to work.

As I locked my front door, I glanced up at a small security camera I had installed in the second-level hallway. I could not be careful enough. Working at Wotherspoon required me to perform some, shall we say, dubious tasks. I had made enemies and took the issue of security seriously.

I rushed to work as fast as I could. Wotherspoon and Associates was located in a formidable glass-and-steel skyscraper just off Park Avenue. It was a veritable fortress complete with armed guards and iris recognition just to get in. I always took the stairs to the fifth floor, where the associates were congregated.

Once there, I made my way through a stormy sea of type A's, including the secretaries. My tiny, windowless office was located in the back. The office was bleak. Piss-colored walls, awful blue carpet dating back to the '70s, and the distinct smell of an aged space. The only thing that livened it up was my golden name plate that read "CAMERON D. STERLING, ESQ." All the associates had the same kind of offices, and we never met clients in them. We steered them to a magnificent meeting room on the fourth floor.

I didn't mind my working environment because I had a plan. I was determined to make partner at any cost. I was going to make it to the legendary twenty-sixth floor, the one that most associates had only heard about. Only a select few ever saw it. And I was going to be one of those lucky ones who did. This measly office was a mere stopgap along the way.

***

The day was progressing uneventfully. I was finding myself in a state of boredom with no conflict to engage in. That is when Linda, the founding partner's stern secretary, came to my door. Linda looked like a creature from some old fairytale, and I would not have been surprised to find out that she transformed into a troll at night.

The old hag walked in without even so much as knocking and said, "Mr. Wotherspoon requests your immediate presence."

She could have just called my desk, but the partners liked to put on a show and strike occasional fear in the fifth-floor associates. Now my office reeked of her. I said to the dragon lady, "I will be up immediately."

Linda went back to the hole she climbed out of. I then made myself more presentable for the partners. I swished mouthwash, spritzed some cologne, and double checked the shine on my shoes. I opted for the elevator instead of the stairs so no trace of perspiration would be seen on me.

When the elevator doors opened, it was like I had entered another world. The twenty-sixth floor was a tribute to lavishness and greed. Linda appeared out of nowhere and led me to an oak-paneled conference room. I was grimly greeted by a room of astute but foreboding older men—the partners. Lurking in a dark corner was an intense-looking man in a well-tailored suit. He was definitely *not* a partner.

Mr. Wotherspoon did not rise out of his chair. His beaky nose reminded me of a bald eagle, and his salt-and-pepper hairline receded all the way to his nape. To compensate, Wotherspoon wore the rest of his hair long and oiled back. With clasped fingers he studied me for a few moments before offering me a seat. I sat at one end of the table alone, while he and all the partners grouped at the other.

"So this is the incredible Cameron Sterling I have been hearing so much about," said Mr. Wotherspoon. He really was not impressed.

"Yes, sir. I have been working here for the past five years, and they've been good ones too. I don't think I would have been requested for this meeting if they had been otherwise."

Mr. Wotherspoon cracked a small smile. He was pleased with my response. "You remind me of myself so many, many years ago. Let's hope for your sake that my impression is correct."

"I have never failed this company. I know you are probably well aware of my record," I said.

Mr. Wotherspoon slid a brown file all the way down the length of the table. "We have been eyeing you for a long time."

I opened the file. It was a case that I had worked on two years earlier. I was hungry to make a name for myself and did some unethical, possibly illegal, moves to get my guilty client off. I had no regrets about it. After all, it was part of my plan to make partner. Now the partners were bringing it back up. Was I about to be fired? I decided to play it cool. "Yes, the Dawson case. Fraud. As I recall, I kept our client out of prison."

"Yes, yes, you did," Mr. Wotherspoon said. I waited for the backlash. But I got another response from him instead. "You did an outstanding job. Just the type of man we consider for a partner."

I tried to maintain my composure, but inwardly I was turning flips. "You're making me a partner?"

"No, not right now. This is a chance to move up, after being thoroughly vetted. As you already know from working on the fifth floor, some of our clients do not possess the best characters. However, the clients that the twenty-sixth floor deals with are of a particular nature. They are some of the world's most elite who may be involved in terrible, even horrific, activities. It is our job to protect them. Sometimes shortcuts have to be taken to please the client. And if that's not enough, more severe methods have to be employed."

Another partner, Mr. Slezak, pointed his stubby finger at the off-putting man who was still standing in the corner. I could make out the faint outline of a large pistol under the silent one's jacket. Mr. Slezak's lips curled into a reptilian smile. "That is Xander. He handles those situations for us."

Xander was a freak of nature. The golem stood inches taller than me and was so massive that his footsteps could leave imprints in the pavement. His freckled, bald scalp unflatteringly showcased his apish, inclined forehead and Quentin Tarantino-like projected chin. His eyes had a color unlike any I had ever seen before—red as rage—and their scorching gaze singed my skin. Xander just stared at me as though his sixth sense alerted him that I was some sort of threat.

Regardless of Xander's mammoth proportions and antisocial personality, I was not intimidated and boomeranged his stare right back at him. It was more than clear that the beastly asshole had no intentions of becoming best buds with me. But obviously Xander had no clue who he was messing with. Fuck him.

"So do you understand what we are *really* all about? What we do here and why?" Mr. Wotherspoon asked me.

I casually responded, "When it comes down to it, are there really such things as right and wrong? Everything is subjective, and we all do what we feel is necessary to reap maximal benefit. Therefore, I completely understand why the firm has to take such drastic measures to protect its interests. It would be foolish not to."

"Well, that brings up another question. Will you be faithful to the firm, or will you backstab us to, as you say, reap maximal benefit? Loyalty to the firm is paramount, Mr. Sterling, and is the only way to a partnership."

I was not a joiner by nature, but I was not about to let them know that. I told Mr. Wotherspoon what he wanted to hear. "I do not have a heart. And I lost my soul a long time ago. I don't mind getting dirty. My dedication to Wotherspoon and its purpose knows no bounds."

The partners contained their delirium at my answer. But I could tell that they were practically skeeting in their pants.

However, Xander and I locked eyes once again. I knew he saw
through my bullshit and had just waged a silent war on me.
That was cool. I had my battle gear on and was ready to rock.
It was definitely on.

Mr. Wotherspoon leaned in. "Now that you are in the fold,
we'd like to bring you in on a unique case. Our client is an
extremely famous and wealthy man who is being extorted for
money."

"Who is the extortionist, and what is the basis for the
extortion?" I asked.

"Because of the extreme sensitivity of the case and because
you are new to the fold, you will only know the extortionist by
the code name Z. As far as the basis for the scheme, that will
be kept among the partners. You will only be handling some
of the lighter aspects of the financials. Securing property assets
and shuffling monies to offshore accounts."

"Why go through all this trouble? Why not involve law
enforcement? Blackmail is illegal."

"Mr. Sterling, Wotherspoon and Associates does have an
extensive network of, shall we say, insiders and helpers in the
police department. However, there are many who are not on
our side. Unfortunately, the allegations about our client are
true, and he would rather not touch Z or…"

Mr. Wotherspoon looked at Xander then continued, "…or
have Z silenced in any way. Our client is covering his behind,
though."

Mr. Slezak gave his two cents. "The firm's retainer is in the
high seven figures. The client is serious about making sure Z
does not go public because it would destroy him, and even our
law firm, if the accusations ever came out. But Z's demands are
becoming excessive."

I knew that this client was just a test to see whether or not my moral compass was broken beyond repair. And indeed it was.

"When do I start?" I said.

"Tonight. There is a gala, and you will be in attendance." Mr. Wotherspoon waved a ticket and passed it down through the line of partners to me. "You will be formally introduced to the client there."

I hated parties, but I hated my for-shit office even more. I read the ticket and recognized the name of the client straight-away—Sig Krok. Fuck. What the hell did he do to warrant all this subterfuge? Not that it mattered. If Mr. Krok fucked up then it was my right to profit from his mistake. I was going to work my ass off on Siggy's case and get that corner office—no matter what. Even if I had to wear a monkey suit and parade around a room full of asses to get it.

Then one of the demon extras from *Hellraiser*—affection-ately known as Linda—came in with a magnum of champagne. As I made small talk with the partners, she dutifully retrieved long-stemmed flutes and poured copious amounts of libation for all, even for herself. Everyone raised their glasses as a wel-coming gesture toward me.

Shit, yeah, I am so fucking in there.

Chapter Four

I had taken too many antidepressants that day, trying desperately to drown out the voice that had been running through my head: *Tonight they are going to figure you out. That you are nothing but a fake. A piece of shit.*

The gala was being held at the famed Demeure de Rêve Hotel. I insisted that Sig book the presidential suite to avoid us having to arrive by limousine. I had too many close calls where I nearly tripped trying to step out of limos in front of a plethora of reporters and photographers. No way was I risking that tonight.

Before the nearly two hundred guests arrived, I went down to survey the ballroom. Frantic decorators, sound people, and caterers scrambled about, putting on the finishing touches.

The ballroom was a perfect analogy of me. It was basically a blank and hollow cavern that only came to life when someone else's vision filled it. As it was fluffed and prepped, the ballroom was transforming into a mirage. That mirage would bring people to it and fool them into thinking it was something that it was not. At the end of the night, after all the guests had gone home, the adornments would be removed. And the ballroom would once again be downgraded to nothingness. Then it would wait, wait, and wait some more until it needed to "become" again.

I looked over at the staircase that I was to descend later that night. To someone else, this whole spectacle would have been perceived as an honor. However, I was terrified that I was going to fumble in front of all those people. I envisioned toilet paper on my shoe, a sneaky booger hanging out of my nose, or an accidental slippage of noxious gas from the bean burrito I had for lunch.

But even worse was contemplating the fact that in a few short hours I would be standing in front of a roomful of critical silhouettes, staring at me with expectations of perfection that no mere human could live up to. They wanted a goddess, and that desire was my fault really. I had manufactured a brilliant lie. The caricature that these people knew, I created with an airy template of illusion. Then Sig came along and grew it to epic proportions. He smelted me like lead in a blast of fire.

The denizens of the glossy world I occupied had everything money could obtain. Yet they still needed something to aspire to and help them forget the emptiness they had inside of them. Like I had inside of me. That's why I was adored by them. They lived vicariously through me, feeding off the illusion that they thought was my life. Their insatiable hunger to consume every part of my existence gave them purpose. Otherwise they had nothing else. There is only so much shopping and yacht hopping you can do before it becomes tedious. After you have bought and seen everything, what else is there? The only thing left is to cannibalize another's life. A life that *seems* to have the one thing they do not: happiness.

They did not want me, not really. The *real* me, that dirt-poor girl who had terrible things happen to her. The girl that was running from the shadows of her past. The girl who was just trying to forget the violation brought upon her. That girl... they would have kicked her in the teeth.

My problem was that even though I knew their love was false, I fed off of them as much as they fed off me. I liked the rush I received from their superficial compliments and jealous stares. It was sick, I know. But I was addicted to it.

So tonight I would once again put on my costume of the glamorous, deliriously happy girlfriend of one of the most powerful men in the world. In return, I would be energized by the crowd falling at my feet. And for a little while, I could forget everything.

The antidepressants started kicking in. Like an actress getting into character, I succumbed to my alter ego. As my body became possessed by her, it felt like she was falling rain, drenching me. I found myself smiling and seducing invisible people. I stood a little taller, my head raised high, and started to walk like Jean-Paul, my Pilates instructor. I was no longer that pathetic girl from Santee, California. I was now the goddess.

Despite that feeling, I still counted the steps on the staircase to make sure I did not trip on my way down. I was not about to be ass out on Page Six.

———

This is some motherfucking bullshit. If I didn't have such a hard-on to make partner, I would not have been caught dead in a wackadoo place like this.

As soon as I stepped into the ballroom, a wave of techno funk assaulted my ears. At three thousand dollars a ticket, you would think they would have had better music. Flashy projected images splashed over every available surface in the chasmal hall. As I went deeper into hell, I was engulfed by purple-hazed celebrities, sugar babies showing off the breast implants sugar daddies had purchased, Andy Warhol wannabes, and gay men decked out in the latest Klå low-rise skinny jeans. Male performance artists hung from the rafters like trapeze artists, wearing only body paint. And I sure as shit wasn't down for that.

Mind you, I knew fashion types were quirky, but this dung was ridiculous. My basic tuxedo made me stand out like Einstein at a monster truck rally.

The light was low, and I could barely see. Plus I had no clue where to go in this madness. I saw none of "my kind" anywhere in the room. I steeled myself and braved the gauntlet through the throbbing crowd, hoping to run into a partner and not giving a damn about who I bumped into along the way. Fuck, I would have been glad to see Stonehenge Linda at that point. But with no partners in sight, all I could think to do was get to the bar.

I'm missing a champion MMA fight for this ridiculousness. Damn it, I sure as hell better make partner for having to endure this.

The crowd definitely had the appearance of eccentricity. But it was not genuine. They were all a bunch of rich bitches who feigned eccentricity because it was en vogue. I had no respect for these poseurs and their obnoxious display of wealth. I was a blue-collar boy and never lost sight of the fact that I had to work harder than everyone else, especially these trust-fund babies.

I finally made it to the bar and plopped down on the stool, which was in the shape of a giant hand with the middle finger sticking up that curled between the legs, grazing my cock. *Really? No, seriously. Really?* I thought as I face palmed and shook my head.

"What would you like, sir?" the flirty, tranny barkeep asked. He kept winking at me like he had a tic.

Dude, you are so barking up the wrong tree.

"Orange juice. Two cubes of ice," I said as I looked back at the retarded extravaganza of flesh behind me. Suddenly the music stopped and "ahhhs" filled the room. All eyes were trained on the staircase. The DJ put on some hip but more sophisticated music.

Sig descended the stairs. He was dressed in all white, which did nothing to flatter his cyanic skin. His face contorted as he forced himself to put on what he considered to be a smile. He looked more constipated than anything. However, he was holding the hand of a radiant creature. She practically glowed with the ethereal haze of a soft-focus lens.

The crowd moved in front of me, blocking my view of the enchanting creature that had mesmerized everyone in the room. I stretched my neck to get a better look. The drag queen announcer chimed in over the microphone. "Please, everyone, give a raucous round of applause to Sig Krok and his lovely girlfriend, Lilly Amsel!"

Lilly? Nah, it couldn't be the same woman from the gym.

My eardrums nearly popped from the astounding volume of claps and cheers. Mind you, I have never behaved like a groupie. But for some reason I, too, was drawn to the mystery woman named Lilly, even though I could not make out the details of her face. In the nebulous light, I could make out long ringlets as they cascaded down her small, bare shoulders and her full, rouge lips that she swiped with her tongue, tantalizing the swooning crowd. She swung her hips like a water snake swimming in a pond as the long train of her dress slithered behind her.

Sig and Lilly stopped near the bottom of the staircase as the spotlight's orb encompassed them. As her face illuminated, I realized it was the same Lilly. She was so shatteringly gorgeous that I almost had to divert my eyes, like I was looking directly into the sun. I was so affected that I had not even noticed that I let my hand fall to my side, and my watered-down juice had spilled onto the floor. Then I heard a finger snap in my head: *Fucker, wake up! You have never been giddified over any woman in your entire life. Don't start that whack shit now.*

I shook my head, trying my damnedest to shake off my spontaneous crush. But I had to admit that it was one hell of a coincidence seeing Lilly there. The mind chatter was relentless: *Is this what kismet means? No way. Cam, just nix that crazy thought. There is no possibility of this moment being fated. It is just mere chance.*

That's what I told myself. But why did it feel like my stomach was collapsing to the ground at the very sight of this woman? I tried to fight it, but my body turned itself and forced my eyes to follow her around the room.

I watched her flit from guest to guest, lilting fake laughs. She was so pretentious. She made sure she touched every shoulder as if she were implanting the guests with the idea of worshipping her. She made her way to the stage area, where two large thrones awaited her and Sig. She had an assistant swoop her train out of the way as she propped herself on the throne, where she would oversee her subjects.

Oh, yeah. Now I remember why I didn't like that girl.

Lilly was just like all the rest of these phonies. I turned to the barkeep. "I'll have a scotch on the rocks."

"What kind of rocks would you prefer?"

"Just give me the damn drink."

I was contemplating leaving when I heard a loud clang behind me. Apparently the hapless waitress dropped her tray and splattered the floor with hors d'oeuvre and canapés. By this time Sig had taken the throne next to Lilly and was glaring down at the waitress, seething. I was waiting for sparks to fly out of his eyes. However, Lilly, in all her grandeur, rushed down to the waitress without hesitation. She squatted down and helped the profusely apologetic woman.

Well, I'll be damned. I would have never pegged Lilly as, dare I say, a caring person.

Then I looked at Sig again. Though he was trying to save face, any discerning person could pick up that he was livid. How dare his girlfriend, as a reflection of him, downgrade herself to the level of a servant? Sig yanked her up by one arm, all while maintaining his smiling social front. He was not about to let the guests see him lose his cool.

Sig straightened up Lilly's mussed dressed and proceeded to parade her around the room like his pet, asserting his dominance over her. There was so much coldness between them that I caught a case of frostbite just watching.

I saw an invasive television crew materialize out of the crowd. The aggressive reporter first put the microphone near Sig's mouth as the partygoers surrounded the couple. Sig gave the female reporter a feral snarl. The reporter quickly backed down and went after the less threatening target. She put the microphone so close to Lilly's mouth it looked like she was about to give it some head. Lilly remained classy, though. As the reporter still held the microphone, Lilly smoothly grasped it and slyly moved it to a more appropriate position.

"Ms. Amsel, you were nothing when you met Mr. Krok. Just a fledging model with a stagnant career. Why do you think a phenomenon like Sig Krok would take on a woman like you?"

As a man, if Lilly were my woman, I would have cursed that reporter bitch out. But Sig was not me. In fact he appeared to relish the reporter's degrading question. I could tell he enjoyed bringing Lilly down. Fortunately for Lilly, an eager autograph seeker—who was refused by Sig—got her off the hook. As she signed the autograph book, Lilly was thinking. She came back at the photographer and said, "I may have felt like you did when you were caught sucking your married boss's dick. Remember the scandal? I do. And look at you now, promoted from the mail room to primetime reporter. Begging *me* for an interview."

I felt like I needed a bowl of popcorn as I watched the volley. The reporter raised her sliver of an eyebrow and went back to Sig. Sig was more receptive this time as he was more on the reporter's side than Lilly's.

"So, Mr. Krok, you are now looking for the new spokes-model for Klå. It seems obvious to use Lilly," the reporter said as she looked Lilly up and down. "But youth is so valued in the industry, and Lilly is quickly approaching her peak. Are you looking for something new? Or will nepotism win out?"

Lilly and the party guests anxiously waited for Sig's response. He looked at the crowd and gave a teasing, sinister grin that he believed was charming.

The reporter pressed on. "What about Jacob Boyd?"

Even from where I was standing, I could see Lilly's countenance drop at the mere mention of the name. Jacob was a tow-haired, cornpone model from Idaho. Only seventeen, the young man was as ruthless and ambitious as I was. He was Lilly's nightmare, her shadow. He was young and tender, while she was becoming an artifact in the modeling world. He worked his way to his current position having been a model since the age of three. Lilly never earned anything; she only slept her way to the top. He was brimming with hubris. She was simply a wreck.

I watched Jacob as he watched Lilly. He had that look. A look I recognized from my own face. The look of a professional chess player contemplating the board for his next move. Jacob was raving with the idea of usurping Lilly's position. There was nothing he would not do to bring her down. That is how I operated daily in my own career.

Just when the theatrics were getting good, my posse from Wotherspoon showed up…fashionably late, of course. I waved my hand in the air so they could locate me.

"Cam, I was hoping I'd see you mixing with the crowd," Mr. Wotherspoon said, somewhat miffed.

"I was just finishing my drink."

He directed me to put my glass down. "No, it is time for business."

I was not about to be punked. I said, "We would not want good scotch to go to waste, now would we?" I finished my drink like a boss.

From that moment on, Mr. Wotherspoon had two thoughts about me. One, I was someone he needed because of my obvious pomposity and proven skill. Two, he would have to watch me carefully because I was not a whipping boy. I knew I had to tread lightly, though. I had no love for Mr. Wotherspoon or the partners, but I needed them to achieve my goal. Wotherspoon and Associates was considered one of the top law firms in New York. If you made it there, you practically had the key to heaven. I had already invested time and was not going to let that hard work go to waste. But there was one other thing. The partners at Wotherspoon were dangerous, and I did not want to be on the receiving end of one of their plots.

Though I was no one's lap dog, I decided that I would be cooperative tonight. But there would only be so much of this subordinate crap I would take. I would play the game; it would not play me.

I could not believe Sig did not stand up for me with that reporter.

What am I saying? I really should *not* have been surprised. He has never been my protector, just my money.

Sig used me too. Before I came into his life, he had a butt-wretched reputation. Klå only survived because of the people who worked under its brand; it had nothing to do with him. Sig's personal popularity grew only because of me.

We met at a modeling shoot. He came over to me and rolled some pinched flesh from my side between his fingers. His first words to me were, "You're too fat. Next." And that was after I had starved for two weeks for that shoot and was just over one hundred pounds. Sig chose another young woman, who eventually ended up dying from anorexia a year later.

When Sig told me I was fat, I pretended it did not bother me. I projected the bubbly "artificial" me instead. As I left the photo shoot, Sig noticed how people were drawn to me, or rather what they thought was me. I was putting on airs of course, but Sig did not know that. He saw an opportunity and had his people call me the next day. We went out on a date. The paparazzi went insane. Sig was instantaneously popular all because I humanized him. His brand's sales soared out of the stratosphere. I moved in so he could so-called mentor and keep tabs on me. I had dated successful men in the past, but Sig was on another level. I became a deity just like him. When the worshippers adored me, it was great. But that feeling came at a tremendous cost. I was doomed to be forever flawless on the surface because I was such a mess underneath.

And now I was at this gala. I saw Sig's attorneys walking toward us. I knew Sig was having some kind of legal issue, but he never revealed to me exactly what it was. I assumed the problem centered on his factory in Thailand, which was mired in a child-labor controversy. But I noticed another face with the usual attorneys. It was Cam from the gym.

The asshole? You have got to be motherfucking kidding me.

I made the mistake of locking eyes with Cam. Oh my fucking God, it was like his eyes had the gravitational force of black holes. I could not help but be sucked in by them. I shuffled on my feet because my naughty bits felt like they were being pierced with a horny spear. Sweat spurted out of my pores, and my extremities tingled. My breathing became staggered as I fought off hyperventilation.

As Cam got closer, I could tell he knew who I was too. He was still looking squarely at me. I could not make out if he was pleasantly surprised or disappointed to see me. The attorneys made their way onto the stage where Sig and I were. Cam definitely stood out among the decrepit-looking crew of older men. Introductions were made, with Cam and I making acquaintances last.

"Hello…Cameron," he said as he took my hand. He had a very strong handshake but was trying his best to be gentle with me.

"Lilly. Lilly Amsel. Nice to meet you. Well, officially. We met earlier. At the elevator."

"I know. I remember. I definitely remember."

Cam and I stood there looking at each other and holding our handshake too long for Sig's comfort. Sig pointed his spindly finger at Cam and asked Wotherspoon, "Who is this man?"

"Cam will be handling the financial aspects of the case," answered Mr. Wotherspoon. "Only the financial aspects."

Sig narrowed his eyes. "I hope he has full understanding of the type of privacy I require."

"He has been vetted," said Mr. Slezak.

I did not hear a word Sig and those old coots were saying. I was too entranced by Cam. I could not believe how he went from that grungy guy at the gym to this exceptional, powerful man. He was filet mignon on a platter, and I was starving. That piece of meat stood in front of me in his perfectly tailored ebony suit. I know it was tacky of me, but I had to examine his shoes. Shoes reveal a lot about a man. If he had on a great suit but his shoes were run-over, it meant he was a fraud. And I was an expert at fraud. I took a slick look down and was able to breathe a sigh of relief. Cam was wearing Allen-Edmonds in basic black, perfectly shined and unscuffed.

Cam might actually be the real deal. But that remains to be seen. He may be crafting an illusion just like me. But, goddamn, if it is an illusion, it's sexy as hell.

Suddenly I heard a familiar voice chirp up. It was Tamara. "Lilly, darling, let's go take some pictures of you mingling with the crowd."

"Well, it was nice seeing you…again," I said to Cam.

"Likewise."

I stepped down into the throbbing crowd. I dared not look back at Cam for fear that Sig would see. I pretended like everything was normal and took the photos Tamara requested. Even though her flash nearly blinded me at times, I managed to make her shots look impromptu and candid.

Still, I could see Cam out of the corner of my eye. I was impressed by his body language as he spoke to Sig. His back was pencil-straight, and his demeanor was that of a person to be reckoned with. Most other people cowered in Sig's presence. Not Cam. His stance let Sig know not to fuck with him.

Sig, on the other hand, fidgeted ever so slightly. I had never seen him do that before.

Tamara had taken hundreds of pictures of me, and I was exhausted from all the posing. Not only that but I had talked so much that my voice was growing raspy. Normally the energy of others fills me up, but right then I was spent. Sometimes it really does take a lot out me to become that other person. I needed a momentary escape from the ballroom to recharge.

I happened upon a secluded balcony. I was fully expecting to come upon a couple of lovers having a tryst, but it appeared to be empty. I was greeted by one of the largest, brightest full moons I had ever seen. It looked like it was so close that I actually reached out to touch it. I laughed at myself, thinking that was so silly.

The air was cold and brisk. It smelled like New York City. I could not help but take a deep, loud breath. At the top of my inhale, I heard someone clearing his throat. Someone had been watching me the whole time, and I was terribly embarrassed. I quickly turned around to apologize for interrupting someone else's private time.

"Oh, I'm so sorry. I was just going back inside."

Cam emerged from the darkness. "No, it's okay. It's refreshing to see someone truly enjoying themselves and our wonderful city."

I did not feel any more tension being around Cam. I was really quite comfortable. I passed him a smile and asked, "What are you doing out here? I thought you'd be talking shop with Sig and the Wotherspoon crew."

"I've been out here for a while now. No disrespect but I had my fill of the fake crowd."

Oh, my God, is he really talking about me?

Cam went on. "You look like you've had enough too."

I realized that this man was under the impression that I was more composed than I really was. A rush of insecurity flooded my brain. I felt the pressure to morph into the centered woman he thought he was talking to.

"I know exactly how you feel. Trust me, it isn't easy being around phonies."

Did I really just say that? Why am I lying to this man? I side-glanced the night sky just to make sure a bolt of lightning was not about to strike me.

Cam took a step closer to me and then leaned over, resting his lower arms on the bannister. "So you and Sig…how long have you been dating?"

Wow. Cam was flirting and feeling me out. My heart pattered as I blushed.

"For a while now."

"A while. Is it serious?"

"As it can be."

"Either you are serious, or you aren't." He inched closer to me. "I don't get the feeling that you're happy."

"Well…"

I hemmed and hawed. I did not want to acknowledge the painful truth about me and Sig and was incredibly unnerved by the questions. I did feel *something* for Sig after all. He provided me with a mansion, opportunities, and more cash than I could spend. I was able to socialize with people others found untouchable. Mind you, the sex was meh, but I never thought about cheating.

I did not have to answer Cam's question thanks to one of Sig's random assistants who had come to drag me back to the gala. I told him I would be in, and then he went back inside.

"Guess I've got to go," I said. And this was good. Not answering Cam's questions added to my mystique.

Cam did not respond. He just stared at me for a moment like he was trying to figure out my deal. "Guess you'd better go then," he said.

I turned and started to walk away but stepped on the train of my dress. I wobbled as I was about to fall to the concrete. Cam dashed over and caught me in his muscular arms before I hit the ground.

He cradled me near his chest. "Are you okay?"

I could smell the musky aroma of his aftershave. "Yes, yes. Thank you."

But there was something else. I felt Cam's massive, thick erection as he pressed against me. He gave me a mischievous grin and pulled me even closer, not embarrassed in the least. I gulped hard and clenched my thighs as my insides released their moist and sticky dew. Panic mixed with desire set in. "I've got to go. Right now," I said, trying not to groan.

Cam took his time letting me go and then handed me my train. "Be careful. It would be a shame to damage something so beautiful."

Oh, no, he didn't.

Blood rushed to my face, which felt like it had been set on fire, and my head started to spin. But after I already made a fool of myself by nearing falling on my ass, I was not going to spaz out again. With all the sophistication I could muster, I gave Cam a sincere and classy thank you.

As I crossed the threshold, I looked back at Cam. His back was leaning against the bannister with his arms stretched to the sides, holding the bars, and his legs crossed at the ankles. He was relaxed, confident. He knew he had something I wanted. His body had become an open invitation for sex. It took all my effort to turn away from that possibility and go back inside.

I reentered the gala feeling rejuvenated and took my place next to Sig. It suddenly felt a hundred degrees hotter in the room. As I fanned hard, Sig noticed that I was smiling a tad bit more than usual.

Suspicious, he asked, "What in the hell is wrong with you?"

"Nothing," I responded coyly. "Absolutely nothing."

Chapter Five

I was absolutely fucking floaty, buzzing around that ballroom like I had taken a few tokes of a fatty. The encounter with Cam left me high as hell, and I wondered if anyone else noticed that my feet were not touching the ground. Somehow osmosis occurred, and some of Cam's essence had sunk into me. With his juice I did not even have to pretend to be charming. I was disarmingly funny, calming, and enjoyable. I was in the zone. However, I kept a watchful eye on the balcony. I did not want to miss it when Cam came back in.

Cam strolled back into the party after a long while. He immediately fixed his steady gaze on me as he circled the room, taking slow and deliberate steps. He made sure to stay in the dark outer fringes of the grand ballroom. He was a lion on the hunt, and I was the helpless gazelle trying to hide in the tall grasses of people. Sometimes he was motionless and faded into obscurity. Other times he appeared virtually out of nowhere, putting me on notice that I was still in trouble. He ghosted his way through the crowd and seemed to be lurking in the background of every spot I treaded in that ballroom.

What was Cam doing? Was he going to take me right in front of Sig? Or would he continue to lie in wait, watching me with those chocolate eyes lined with sooty lashes? I tried to avoid looking directly at him but just could not help it. Those eyes—those dark pools of infinity—were calling me. Beckoning me. Daring me to come back and finish what was started. And I wanted to so very badly. I wanted to feel his hands all over my peachy skin, his tongue probing my welcoming mouth, and his dick deep inside me. But that damn Sig remained leeched onto me, almost as though he knew that someone was going after his woman. More like his property.

Cam lingered while giving me a come-hither stare. He was waiting for me to break away from Sig. He tilted his head toward the hallway. I knew he wanted me to meet him there. Cam then raised his brow and disappeared into the hall.

Sig was engrossed in a conversation with a couple of urolagnia aficionados. Sig had been trying to get me to try watersports. Mind you, he just wanted to pee on me, not me on him. It was just another way for him to control and humiliate me. But the piss-slurping couple he was conversing with offered me a chance to escape to the hallway.

"All this talk about pee is scintillating, really. But if you all would kindly excuse me, I must powder my nose," I said, trying not to look suspect.

Wow! I really said "powder my nose"? Is it 1940? Whatever. Fuck it. Just as long as I can get to that hallway.

Sig gave me a sardonic look. "Can't you wait? We are having a conversation. That wouldn't be polite, now would it? Besides, you could learn a thing or two so that you can stop being so prudish."

"Normally I would not suggest letting a perfectly good golden shower go to waste, but I do understand how uncomfortable it feels holding back the wet works," said the male dressed in the vinyl pants. "Let her go. But next time maybe I can drink it instead?"

"Thank you," I said as I tried not to hurl and get away as fast as I could. But I was stopped by the female half of the pair. "Do you mind if I watch? All you have to do is leave the stall door open. I can just stand there."

"Uh, yeah…I do mind," I said as politely as I could. My legs were suddenly on autopilot, whisking me away from these skeevy pervs.

I hurried to the hallway, still freaked out by the deviants in the other room. I looked back to make sure they were not chasing me with catheters and urine specimen containers. After I had attained a safe distance from the ballroom, wanton anticipation of Cam avalanched me. I could not wait for our two bodies to come together—hard and tight. With my mouth parched, I took another turn in the labyrinth hallway in search of pleasure. The hallway was dimly lit with a few small candle sconces and accented by mahogany wood draped with crimson velvet swags. The drifting scent of Cam's aftershave still hung in the air, and I followed it. Soon the bright lights from the ballroom faded into oblivion.

"Hello? Cam?" I whispered.

There was no answer, yet I was undeterred. Cam's heady scent grew more pronounced; I knew he was close by. I could feel him watching me from the dark. I was vulnerable and maybe a little bit frightened. Not because I thought he would hurt me. But because it had been so long since I felt any sort of bliss—the ecstatic bliss that being with Cam promised—that I feared it might kill me.

"Please stop teasing me, Cam. Come out. You asked, and I came," I begged.

A powerful hand took hold of my arm from behind. I knew

it was Cam by the way my body trembled as if a harsh gust of wind had blown through it.

"Come here, Lilly." The bass of his voice had such resonance that it vibrated the hallway even at a low volume. Cam turned me around. He pulled me toward his body, and I met his embrace. His heartbeat was thumping hard against his chest, so hard it seemed life-threatening. Cam lifted my face to his. His thick lips grazed mine. His nature rose once again, and I knew where this was heading.

I started having second thoughts. I was not a cheat and did ultimately aspire to integrity. I had made a commitment to Sig and took it seriously. What was about to happen was not only wrong but dangerous considering Sig's often sociopathic ways. Cam, however, was unstoppable. His lips glided across my face and down to my neck. I started going limp.

"Cam, I think we should stop. This isn't right," I said with my body giving way to him.

But Cam did not care. He continued to kiss me softly at first, tempering me, because if he had given it all to me at one time, I would have passed out. But he was in control as he kissed me again and again. His heated hands began tracing my curves. At first he started with my shoulders. Then he moved to the dip in my lower back and finally to the round curvature of my bottom. Cam broke lip contact and squatted. Those hands, those massive hands, found their way under my dress and meandered from my ankles to my knees and were heading to my thighs when we heard a rustling in the dark. Cam stood up, and we both peered behind us toward the darkness.

"Lilly!" an angry voice shouted. It was Sig. We could hear him heading straight toward us. I looked back toward Cam, and he was gone. He basically evaporated into the blackness like he was never there in the first place. I turned back, and Sig was standing there leering at me.

"Have you finished pissing yet?"

"Huh?" I said, still dazed by lust.

"Pissed? Have you pissed yet? It is time to go."

"Oh, uh-huh. I...I..." I mumbled. I was so worked up that I did not have enough blood flow to my brain to form a coherent thought. Practically lobotomized, I looked back at the spot where I had last seen Cam, desperately hoping he would reappear.

Sig glowered at me. "You have been acting strange all night. I know you are up to no good. I don't know what it is, but I will find out."

"There is nothing going on. I'm not doing anything wrong." I was a terrible liar and stammered like an idiot. See, this is exactly the scenario I did not want. I had to lie so much when it came to my identity; I did not want to lie about another man too.

I had to leave Cam alone. Being involved with him would only make me more of a fraud than I already was.

Chapter Six

The ride back home was long and quiet. Sig and I sat on opposite sides of the limousine. He looked straight ahead with no emotion. I was still recovering from the rendezvous with Cam. As we crossed the George Washington Bridge, I could see the lights of New York fading fast behind me.

I sighed, knowing that Cam was somewhere in the city. Then it dawned on me that I was sopping wet for a man whose last name I did not even know. I could only grin at myself for being such a fucking slut. But I knew that I could never let that happen again. Not only would that endanger my hard-fought-for relationship with Sig and all the perks that came with it, but I was sure it would have some serious repercussions for Cam as well.

However, there was one perk—the spokesmodel position—that seemed to be just out of reach. There was no way I was going to let that ass wipe Jacob usurp that prize from me. I braced myself to have "the talk" once again with Sig. I had to tread lightly because the last time I brought it up resulted in his having a near-cataclysmic outburst during which he hurled accusations at me, mostly about my nonexistent attempts at trying to control him.

I looked over at Sig. The streetlights incandesced his pale skin, making him glimmer like a freaky glow ball. His blue eyes were so translucent that they blended into the whites, giving him a zombified look. He was a stone monument sitting over there. No animate life seemed to be in him.

"Sig, I need to talk to you about—" I said carefully. Sig, with almost robotic precision, turned to me with eyes totally lacking in expression. He did not even blink. I lost all my nerve as he coldly considered me.

"Never mind. I guess we can talk later," I said, quickly averting my gaze to the darkness whizzing past us. I slumped down into the seat, closed my eyes, and drifted into an unimaginably real fantasy. Images of Cam appeared behind the blackness of my lids. In my dream, whatever Cam had in mind, he wanted to take his time. A long time.

My body relaxed, and I could feel Cam's phantom touch all over again. It was toasty, sensual, and painfully slow. His invisible fingers found their way between my thighs. I squirmed a bit, and Sig thought I was just making myself more comfortable in the seat. No, it was nowhere near comfortable. It was agonizing, this thought of Cam seducing me.

The invisible hand stroked its way to my upper thigh. There, fingers teased the crease between my leg and the outer perimeter of my honey pot. I found myself subtly squirming as my stomach clenched into a knotted fist. Cam's specter finger pulled aside the crotch of my lacy red panties and found its way to my slit. But before it could slide between my pulsing, juicy lips, I was jarred awake by the sound of the gate opening. Sig and I had arrived back home, and the spell was broken.

Our long, gravely driveway twisted through a dense canopy of leafless limbs that hung over the road like gnarly fingers. Heaviness set upon me, bearing down more and more the closer we got to what should have been a romantic fortress. It was simply a prison to me.

The magnificent house came into view. Its opulence was showcased by large floodlights that allowed Sig to behold his trophy even in the darkest of night. The expansive manse was gratuitously modeled after the European castles Sig admired when he was a child. Even though it had spectacular views of the forest, it was ominously isolated from civilization as it sat at the backend of vast acreage.

I thought to myself that I should have been happy. After all, I had willfully social climbed my way here. I did that believing that all the material trappings and lavishness would save me from myself and my past. But they did not. If anything they made it worse because I now knew there was nowhere else to run. I knew one thing, though: that I was not going backward. No matter how shitty Sig was to me, at least I had plenty of money and some notoriety. I could never get those things on my own. As far as I was concerned, there was no other man on earth who could give me those things either. In the end, whatever money and praise from other people could not give me, Prozac and Xanax could, and I was satisfied with that.

Sig got out of the car before I did and went up the stairs without even as much as looking back at me. I could tell the limousine driver was embarrassed for me when he let me out. Ashamed, I could barely look the driver in the eye. He walked me to the door and tilted his head down with respect. I gave him a hefty tip and sent him on his way. As I watched the limousine drive away, I stayed outside for a while. It was frigid out there, yet the temperature did not stop me from stalling. I just could not bring myself to go into the house. However, the howling wind whipped under my dress, and my skin was going numb. I had no other choice than to go inside.

As soon as I got in the door, Sig was on me like a rabid dog. "Close the damn door! You are letting all the heat out. You would think your parents would have raised you better." He then gave me a smug look because he knew what really happened in my upbringing and sometimes used it as ammunition. "Oh, well, considering your folks, I guess you wouldn't have known better."

Sig's cruel laughter echoed relentlessly throughout the hollow house. It was easy for sound to travel through it because of the highly polished marble floors and obvious lack of cushy, soft furniture to absorb it. Being in that house and with Sig vampired out whatever good feelings Cam had given me that night. All I could do was watch as Sig turned away like he did not just sting me and go up one side of the double staircase. Totally defeated, I went up the other side. When I reached the second floor, I trailed behind him like a pitiful little puppy that had just been smacked on the nose.

If people knew what was really going on in our house, they would have wondered why I stayed with Sig. It was really simple. He knew me all too well. He knew all my hopes and dreams and, most important, he knew my secret pain. He used that pain to his advantage, knowing how to sap my power. In that respect he became the embodiment of the pain I was running from. Sadly, I stuck with what I knew. As a little girl, horror came to my room in the wee hours of the night and inflicted such hurt on my body that I splintered. That allowed me to mentally adjust to the torture and function at some level. It was easy to do as long as my boogeyman kept telling me it loved me afterward. Now, fucked-up relationships were the most comfortable for me. Anything else was so foreign that I would not have known how to handle it. Yet I longed for a good relationship all the same.

This left me somewhat schizophrenic. One part of me, a teensy-weensy part, was struggling to be sane. It would ask things like, *What are you doing, Lilly? Why are you here with Sig? Don't you deserve better than this?*

The other part was cray-cray. It had much bigger muscles as if it had been exercising in a prison yard. It would always respond, *No, you don't deserve better. Remember what your father did? That was your fault for letting it happen.*

Suddenly I felt a painful surge of pins and needles, like my whole body had fallen asleep. I knew if I had entertained the thought of my father any longer, I would vomit right then and there. Sig might have conjured him up in my thoughts, but I had to make the decision to block my father out for the rest of the night. For sanity's sake.

I entered the bedroom that I shared with Sig. The room was so like him. It was igloo cold and decorated with metal furniture that was always chilly to the touch. The only fabric in the room was the crisp curtains and stiff bed linen, which were chrome silver. I slipped on my pashmina shawl and sat at my dressing table, where my ever-ready prescription of Klonopin was waiting for me. I stared at the bottle and contemplated not succumbing to it. Despite the relief it gave me, it was only temporary. I longed for an existence where I did not have to be tethered to my medicine cabinet just to function halfway normally. As my hand edged over to the Klonopin, I wondered how other people did it. How did they cope? How did they manage to live life genuinely? Most importantly, how did they have the dumb luck of avoiding the childhood I had?

My hand finally gripped the bottle and opened it. I hesitated, trying so hard not to give in, but I did. I looked at myself in the mirror, once again feeling like a failure. However, I was still relieved that the anxiety would soon be kept at bay.

As I started to unzip my gown, I felt it was just as good a time as any to ask Sig about the modeling position.

"Sig, I don't mean to press but about the spokesmodel position? You haven't made a decision, and I figure I am just as good as anyone else. I would like to be the face of Klå. I have the look and some experience. Sig, really? What are you waiting for?"

Sig smiled as he walked toward me. I was still sitting at my dressing table when he stood behind me and placed his icy hands on my shoulders. I started to think that I must have made a pretty good argument, and he was about to extend some rare kindness by giving me a massage. He touched my skin as I purred and relaxed into his soft strokes.

But as Sig rubbed my shoulders, his hands started to dig into me harder and harder. He suddenly grabbed my chin with one hand, while his fingertips almost pierced my skin with the other.

He spoke in a chillingly calm voice: "You horrid creature. I pulled you out of a trash heap and made you a respectable person. And this is what you do? Give stupid demands to me?" Sig guided my face around the room by my chin and continued with his controlled demolition.

"Look at all of this. This house, these clothes, the jewels. You would not have any of it if it weren't for me. You should be on your knees thanking me for dragging you out of hell and bringing you here, you ungrateful wench." He let my face go with a snappy twist. "When I decide who the face of *my* company should be, I will tell you when I am good and ready."

Sig wiped his hands on his shirt, trying to remove any trace of me off his body. I considered fighting back, but at that moment he looked so much like my father. All I could do was bow out.

Besides, I was already used to the way things were for me. As a child, I got used to being a punching bag. As a teen, I got used to men using me as a sperm receptacle. And in this so-called relationship with Sig, I got used to being treated like fecal matter.

Later that night I woke up from a restless sleep. I was clinging to one edge of the bed with my back turned toward Sig. I listened for the creaky sound of his breathing and did not hear it. I looked back and saw he was not there. The duvet on his side of the bed had not even been pulled back. Something told me to go find him. I quietly rose out of bed and did not even bother putting my silk slippers on. My intuition told me that he was up to no good, and this was a perfect opportunity to catch him in the act.

I went to the hallway and saw the hazy glow of a light coming from down below. I sneaked down the stairs and was for once thankful that the floors were made of marble—no squeaking. I could see that the light was coming from the direction of Sig's office. I tiptoed to the door that he had stupidly left open and peeked in. He was instant messaging someone. From the unusual lusty look on his face, I figured it was some woman, a secret love.

It was not like I had not suspected this. For months Sig had hawked his computer and was skittish whenever I got near it. If I walked into the room, he changed the screen or put the lid down. Mind you, I had seen too many talk shows where an unfaithful lover stored illicit photos or online chat records on their computers or had other suspicious behavior. Sig was following those same patterns verbatim.

But there was more. In the past I had seen way too many semen-crusted tissues piled up in Sig's waste bin next to his desk. Obviously he had a penchant for jacking off at his computer. Shit, there were so many yellowed tissues that Lin, our housekeeper, would not empty the can. And that was her fucking job. However, the thing that caught my attention—more than the trash—was that new, distinct patterns had developed. Whenever Sig got off his computer, each and every time, one of two things would happen. The first thing was that he would want to have sex with me immediately like he had just come home from a strip club and needed a release. I guess whatever images his secret love was sending aroused him so much that not even masturbation could settle him down. He needed a flesh-and-blood body to substitute for his lover. I always acquiesced because I felt I had to pay him back for this lifestyle in some kind of way. I knew that Sig was using my body as a substitute for the person he really wanted to be with.

During those times I could not call what we did love-making, intercourse, or even fucking. It was too clinical for that. Coitus, yeah, that was the best way to describe it. Bland, scientific, matter of fact. Our coitus was always impersonal and doggie style. In that position there is no way to connect because only a couple inches of snatch and dick are involved. I just figured that Sig could not stand looking at my face for some reason.

The other thing that would happen when Sig ended his secret computer romps was that he would become more belligerent or violent than usual. Those were the times he was most pissed that I was not his secret love. He hurled the most disgusting insults at me, so much so that I thought acid was going to drip from my ears. Other times I had to hide bruise marks from the adoring public because of sheer humiliation or for fear of losing my goddess status.

There was a period of time when I was actually bold enough to play private eye. When Sig was gone, I tried to hack into his computer. However, he was paranoid and constantly changed his password. Sig was not a spring chicken, and his memory would blip sometimes. So I knew he had to be keeping a log of passwords. But I could not get into his desk drawer. It was always locked.

I know I should not have cared if Sig was dicking around. He was an asshole. But even though our relationship was strained, my pride could not bear the idea of him cheating on me with another woman. It would only validate all the negative feelings I had about myself. So this night I dealt with it the only way I could. I went back upstairs, climbed into bed, and pretended nothing happened.

But two questions always screamed in the back of my mind: Why didn't Sig just date his secret lover out in the open? Why continue with this sham of a relationship with me?

Sig finally came up about an hour later. He got into bed and nudged me. Out of habit I got on all fours. He mounted me from behind. I could barely feel his reedy penis as he pumped me with no discernible rhythm. It took all of one minute to feel him start to buck, jackrabbit style, and then tense up as he came. His limp dick slacked out of me and was followed by his watery cum sliming down my thigh.

I went to the bathroom to towel off. Sig's nasty cum was already crusting on me. I wiped hard, breaking it into flaky pieces. There was one spot that would not get clean. I wiped harder, reddening my skin, but that cum did not want to come off. Hot water on the towel finally did the trick. I tossed the towel into the hamper and was about to go back into the bedroom. But as I reached for the door, I slumped to the floor and cried instead.

Chapter Seven

I was edgy and rapidly tapping my pencil on top of my aluminum desk. My cell phone was directly in front of me, practically blowing up from a barrage of missed calls and constant texts being sent by Rebecca.

It was a couple of days after the gala, but my mind was still in that hotel hallway. The way I lost control with Lilly was shocking to me. I had never been out of my senses like that before in my entire life. The magic of the night made it seem okay to get swept away in a storm of passion, as though there would be no consequences for making love to her. But on this blustery morning, the cruel, harsh chill of reality stung my face.

I tapped the pencil harder as I tried to disperse my agitation. Oh, Lilly…damn it. What was I supposed to do? Give up everything for a woman I did not even know? For a shot at a relationship? A maybe? A could be? A mere possibility?

Now, the chance to advance at Wotherspoon was real. Hell, it was practically a done deal. I had worked too hard and for too many years to let it slip away from me. So I was thankful that I did not get in too deep with Lilly the other night. I would chalk that whole episode up to experience and put it in my mental bank as a memory that could be pulled up from time to time.

It was now time to regroup and refocus. I had to remember

who I was—a connoisseur of beautiful women. A man who
never had to work to get one as they were always lined up to
have me. I was not the type of guy who went ape shit over a
woman. Those types were weaklings to me. I knew how to stay
in control at all times. And as far as Lilly was concerned, I was
determined to do just that.

I purposefully tried to block out everything that happened
at that party and dive into a stack of Sig's financial records
instead. It was my plan to clear them out by the end of the day.

But thoughts of Lilly distracted me. Trying not to think
about her was like trying not to breathe. There was just something about her. As Lilly flooded my mind, I leaned back
into my seat and reminisced about the velvet softness of her
skin. She smelled like vanilla cream, and I wanted to run my
tongue all over her body, tasting her sweetness. I felt my nature
hardening as I thought about what I would have done to her. I
would have pushed her against the wall, ripped her panties off,
and fucked the shit out of her right then and there. My strokes
would not have been delicate and tender. I would have all but
fucked another hole into her. If Sig had not showed up, that is
exactly what would have gone down. Right then and there, I
made the decision to avoid Lilly Amsel at all costs. I would not
get caught up again.

The sound of my cell phone ringing jolted me back. I
picked it up to look at the screen, and once again Rebecca was
on the other end.

This bitch is fucking batshit crazy.

I momentarily set Sig's financials aside to deal with Rebecca's nonsense by sending her to voicemail and then proceeded
to delete the fifty-two texts she sent me. At message thirty-two,

Robert Thomas knocked on my door as he simultaneously strolled into my office. Robert had been hired by Wotherspoon three years before I was. He had eyed a partnership just like me but had failed to make any progress and could not understand why. I knew. He was a truly decent man who wanted to do and did the right thing *all* the time. At Wotherspoon that was a liability. They gave him softball cases, ones in which being a nice guy would be of no consequence. I liked him. Hell, I fucking admired the guy. He had an average upbringing in every imaginable way. This white-bread background groomed him to only see the world as basically a safe place. He was not bred to have a malicious, ruthless bone in his body. Whenever he was around, I could see what I might have become if I did not have the history that I did.

Robert plopped down in the glorified lawn chair across from me. He had that ever-present goofy, optimistic smile on his face. "Dude, I heard about you being invited to the twenty-sixth floor." Robert started bowing in sarcastic reverence and continued, "You are a god. I am not worthy to share the same air space as you."

I regally lifted my hand, instructing my subject to rise. "Yes, I am spectacular."

Robert and I had a good laugh. He was one of a precious few I could cut loose with. But my tone turned somber. "Things are really intense up there. More ruthless than what I have normally experienced."

Robert looked behind him, making sure no one was within earshot. "Yeah, I have heard rumors of some shady activity up there. Like what happened to Gene Byrd."

"Who's Gene Bryd?"

"I didn't know him that well. He went missing a few days after I started here. He was poised for a partnership, and they say he had to prove himself on some real shady case. Apparently he grew a conscience and tried to get out of it. But the big boys on the twenty-sixth floor weren't having it. Next thing you know, poof. Vanished. Cops were crawling all over this place and questioning everybody. His office mate said that Gene had expressed some fear about whatever case he was working on and accused Wotherspoon and Associates of orchestrating Gene's disappearance. But the only thing Gene was working on was the financials of some oil magnet. What are you working on?"

"Financials."

Robert sucked air through his teeth like he had just been burned by boiling water. "Man, I am not going to tell you how to run your business, but seriously you need to be careful."

I must admit that it was somewhat disconcerting seeing an uncharacteristic grave face on Robert. However, I could not believe that he gave credence to some silly rumor about some missing man. I blew it off and gave him an incredulous look, mostly to set him at ease. I said, "Look, you said it yourself that there was nothing to implicate Wotherspoon in the Bryd disappearance. The story sounds like something a bunch of gossipy secretaries came up with to quell office boredom. Besides, if you truly believed that Wotherspoon was really nefarious, what makes you stay here?"

"It's called a wife, mortgage, and three kids."

"Lucky for me I don't have those problems."

"Hey, watch it now," Robert said jokingly. But then his tone switched back to serious. "No, really. I am here because I have to be. People depend on me. You have created a life where you have no dependencies either on you or you on someone else. So you have choices. I know you want this promotion. Hell, it's like it has been eating away at you for the past few years. But just don't get twisted up in the mentality of the twenty-sixth floor. Despite what you may think, there are other things more important than career success. Trust me; there will be something you will want more. Don't destroy your soul so much with this job that you can't have that other thing."

Robert's words caused my stomach to cinch up into a knot. I knew he was right. Up until the night of the gala, I had never encountered anything I desired as much the Wotherspoon partnership. But Lilly happened into my life, and she was turning it upside down.

I did not have much time to contemplate that matter. Looking past Robert, I could see the crowd of attorneys and secretaries parting like the Red Sea. Mr. Wotherspoon made a god-like appearance to our humble mortal floor with Xander taking up the rear. They were headed directly for my office.

Robert immediately stood up and adjusted his tie. "Uh-oh, Cam. What the fuck did you do?" he whispered.

"I don't know," I said. I stood up and locked eyes with Mr. Wotherspoon but could not read him. He had his same sour face on. I knew he was unsure about me, especially since he saw so much of himself in me.

Now, outwardly I was the picture of self-confidence. Inside, I was like: *Oh, shit! They found out about me and Lilly. This old bastard is about to lay into my ass and fire me. Whatever he says, take it like a man, like you don't give a fuck. Push the papers off the desk and say, Fuck all you mofos! Suck my dick while you're at it. Douches.'* I thought that then I would top it off by throwing my hands in the air and giving them a Kanye shrug.

But I would never do that. That was some sissy shit. No matter what happened, I never let anyone get the best of me.

Except Lilly...God, I really must stop thinking about that woman.

After striking a bit of terror into the rest of the staff, Mr. Wotherspoon finally glided into my office. I heard the smooching sounds of Robert's ass kissing. "Good day, Mr. Wotherspoon. Pleasant weather we're having," he said, cheesing hard.

"It is gray and twenty degrees outside," Mr. Wotherspoon responded, not in the least bit impressed by Robert.

"You're absolutely right, sir. It is a terrible day," Robert corrected.

I could see why Robert had never been invited to the twenty-sixth floor. I liked him, but he was a punk. Xander snapped his finger and pointed at the door, his not-so-subtle way of telling Robert to get the hell out. He was talking incessantly as he stepped back into the main office when Xander slammed the door right in his face. Robert stepped a few feet away, but that did not stop him or everyone else from trying to gawk through the slats of blinds in my office.

Xander pulled out the seat where Robert had been sitting, and Mr. Wotherspoon made himself comfortable in it. "Cam, if you are going to be a partner, you really must disassociate yourself from the likes of Robert."

Still suspicious about the purpose of the visit, I got straight to the point. "So what brings you down here to the fifth floor?"

Mr. Wotherspoon looked at me through a squint. "Mr. Sterling, the name on the front of the building is mine, not yours. I ask the questions around here."

I gave a nod, pretending to agree with his meager display of dominance. This was all still part of the game. And I was an expert player.

Xander placed some documents on my desk as he stared me down. The paperwork was thick and secured in an envelope with a wax seal bearing the imprint of Wotherspoon and Associates.

"You are about to go out to Sig's place for a meeting. Those files...you're taking them with you," Mr. Wotherspoon instructed.

I waited for him to make mention of my improprietous behavior. There was nothing. Then it dawned on me that he said to go out to Sig's place. I knew Lilly would be there. This was not good. I had already decided not to ever make personal contact with her again to avoid a repeat of what happened at the gala. Now they were throwing me back into the lion's den of temptation.

I tried to get out of it. "Mr. Wotherspoon, I have so much work to go through. I think it may be best for a courier to deliver the documents. Better yet, I can send it out by fax personally and meet with Sig another time...in the office."

Mr. Wotherspoon's ears turned an ugly shade of tomato red. He did not like me telling him what could or should be done. He gave me a negative checkmark on his mental list. I was overstepping my narrow boundaries and jeopardizing my promotion.

"The information in this folder cannot be trusted to just

anyone. You *will* deliver it personally." He stood up and started on his way out but not without a final word. "It is too late in the process to replace you. And, unfortunately, I am still intrigued to see how you will manage this case. But if I cannot trust you to be on board with all I request, well, Wotherspoon and Associates will have to deal with you."

I looked at Mr. Wotherspoon, subduing any sort of expression on my face. But I was grinning inside like the Cheshire Cat at his not-so-veiled threat.

No, Mr. Wotherspoon. I will deal with you.

Mr. Wotherspoon and Xander stepped back into the main office. All the office mice once again scurried, pretending to actually be working as not to provoke Wotherspoon's ire.

Still, that envelope loomed large on my desk. I started thinking that there was another way to look at the assignment I had just been handed. Once again circumstances conspired for me to meet up with Lilly. I decided that I would make every effort to resist her first. And after that…well, I would be open-minded and let events occur as they may.

Chapter Eight

Most days I hated being Lilly Amsel, and today that senti-ment was in overdrive.

In a fit of self-loathing, all I could do was just sit on the couch and stare at one of many gigantic portraits of Sig. I thought about getting a pair of scissors and slicing into it. Just ripping it to hell. Even better, throw it on the floor, drop my shorts, and take a big shit all over it, right there in the living room.

I was so grouchy that morning, especially since I woke up with a throbbing tension headache. It did not help that the sunrise could not alleviate the drab gray sky. I tried to get my head together but found that task nearly impossible. Maybe it was PMS. Maybe it was because Sig was meeting with Jacob that morning.

The headache just would not let up. I popped another aspirin and swallowed it dry. I coughed as the pill scraped down my throat, making the headache even worse. I started thinking and came to a realization as to what had caused it to begin with. This excruciating pain made its introduction a few hours after my sidelined tryst with Cam.

Though Sig and I had relations, I had never once cum with him. I just screwed him because it was my duty as a girlfriend. Sig believed himself to be a stellar lover because of my moaning and groaning. I only performed those theatrics to make him cum faster and get the hell off of me. However, I never once thought about cheating. I had no desire to join the ranks of Ashley Madison—until I met Cam.

Ever since the gala, the memory of Cam had me in a state of protracted arousal that could not be satisfied. For the past few days, my crazy headache grew stronger as the blood from my brain pooled to my reawakened pussy. My kitty was so sensitive that I could barely stand wearing panties. I tried to masturbate to relieve the built-up pressure between my legs. I had not masturbated in years and was somewhat embarrassed by it. But something had to be done. Cam's bedroom eyes and chiseled body were my inspiration. I vigorously rubbed my clit whenever I was out of Sig's presence. As visions of Cam fucking me sent me into a frenzy, I came over and over again. Yet I was not satisfied. I knew I needed the real thing to satiate my desire. But I could not have Cam. Being with him was not prudent and just plain wrong.

So I just looked at Sig's nasty-ass portrait instead. I felt a sense of grief over what I had lost to be with him. But I also recognized how far away I was from the dreadful life I had. Even though Sig was a son of a bitch, I was still in a better place than before.

The doorbell rang. This was surprising and upsetting because no visitors were expected today. I was looking like a hot mess in some raggedy cut-off shorts and an old fleece sweatshirt that I had cut the neck out of so it would hang off one shoulder. My messy hair was just thrown into a bun, and I had some toothpaste on a premenstrual zit.

"I'm coming," I said in a frustrated scowl.

As I got closer to the front door, I embraced my body

as a frigid draft from outside seeped in. When I reached the entrance, I stealthily looked outside. In the circle of the driveway, I saw a motorcycle. It looked familiar, but…no…it could not be Cam's. I thought for a few seconds, trying to recollect who Sig knew that drove a Harley. No one. Sig's crowd only knew how to hail taxis or ride in the back of limousines. I reasoned it must have been someone who lost their way or an overzealous fan of Sig's.

I opened the door, and standing before me was a tall figure taking off his motorcycle helmet. I thought I would stop breathing when it was revealed to be Cam. I closed my eyes, not believing my wet dream was standing before me in the flesh.

He's not really here. It's just the Prozac. You have got to get off that shit.

My eyes slowly opened to give the illusion time to slip away. However, Cam was still there. And, Sweet Jesus, he was looking so fine.

Cam ran his fingers through his hair, tamping it down after it had become mussed by his helmet. He had on basic jeans that accentuated his athletic frame and black boots. As he unzipped his weather-worn coat, he passed me an easy grin. "Well, if it isn't Miss Lilly Amsel. Can't say that I am disappointed to see you."

I stood there dumbfounded for about two seconds until abject horror consumed me. Cam had a way of reducing me to a blubbering fool. Whenever I was around him, I lost all of my contrived sophistication and fell back into my old trailer-park ways. It also dawned on me that while this man was standing there looking like walking sex, I looked like I could spoil milk.

I had not showered and probably still had the crust in the corners of my mouth from last night's sleep. I felt incredibly vulnerable without the crutch of cosmetics on my pale face.

Omigod! Did I put on deodorant? Shit!

I realized that I had not said a word to Cam yet when he put his fists—one of which held a folder—to his mouth and blew on them to keep warm.

"Cam, what are you doing way out here?"

"I'm here to see Sig and deliver these papers."

"Sig isn't here and didn't mention you were coming. He's in the city."

Cam looked past me like he wanted to come in. As I surveyed his body, I wanted him to come in too. My eyes made it back to his, and we made deep contact. I then noticed that Cam was sneaking peeks at my chest. I glimpsed down and saw that my nipples were rock hard, enlarged, and pointed straight at him. Normally I would attribute my gigantic niblets to the freezing temperature, but it was Cam. He just made me cock hungry. Cam, meanwhile, slowly ran his tongue across his top lip as if he were goading me to let him do that to my tits.

"I'm sure he won't mind if I come inside," Cam said. "Please let me inside."

I shivered as he moved closer to me. "No, I don't think it would be wise to have you come into my house. I mean, not while Sig is away. Especially after what happened between us the other night."

Cam played dumb. "The other night? Elaborate."

"You know exactly what I'm talking about."

"Hey, I'm just here to deliver papers. But, still, being inside would be so nice."

Aw, damn it with the double entendres.

Yes, I wanted Cam to *come* inside. But I also did not want to piss Sig off. And Sig would definitely be pissed if he knew Cam was there unsupervised. I just could not risk alienating my benefactor for a quick screw. Moreover, I knew that if Cam crossed that threshold, my whole world would be sent into a maddening tailspin.

However, my libido found a way to convince me that it was okay for Cam to be there. I said, "It would be a shame for you to travel all this way just to turn right back around. Come in. Maybe Sig will return while you're here. I'm only letting you in because of him."

Cam gave me a "yeah, right" chuckle and strutted in. He smelled like the outdoors, the scent of winter crispness perfectly combined with slight mustiness. As he went past me, I caught sight of his ass. His jeans were somewhat fitted and hugging his butt. The seam journeyed along his ass crack, delightfully separating the buttocks and displaying their definition. They were firm and slightly rounded. I could tell that ass could deliver a powerful thrust. Cam turned around and caught me watching his behind. I tried to save face.

"The papers…you can put them in the living room." I pointed him toward it then watched him strut confidently into the living room. He walked like a king. His shoulders were large and square, while his gait was purposeful. He dropped the papers on a large table with a thud that echoed through the hollow room. Cam strode back in my direction. I was nervous and felt my heart start to flutter. "Coffee? I can have the housekeeper brew some up. Want some?" I said, scurrying past him.

Of course Cam mischievously grinned and said, "Sure do."

He walked behind me on our way to the kitchen. He made me feel so self-conscious. I could feel his lustful gaze traveling all over my body. Hell, I even heard a low growl come out of his mouth. I could not get to that kitchen quick enough.

After we entered the kitchen, I immediately directed my faithful housekeeper, Lin, to prepare Cam a robust cup of coffee as it was obvious he would not tolerate a weak brew. Lin, through a heavy Chinese accent, said, "What kind of coffee would you like?"

Cam's face was totally perplexed. "Just coffee, I guess."

I watched Lin go to the hutch and open it. The inside was stocked with the best and most expensive coffees from around the world. Cam looked upon them with confusion washing over his face. Cam was a store-brand kind of man; Folgers was the good stuff to him. Perplexed, he looked at me, shaking his head.

Tickled, I said, "Fazenda Santa Ines seems about right for you. It comes from South America—Brazil, in fact. It is sweet, lemony, and clean in its taste. Lin will make it extra strong just for you."

"Since when do people need passports just to drink coffee?" Cam joked.

Lin ground the beans and set the pot to drip. Then I dismissed her so Cam and I would have some time alone. I always enjoyed feeding a man but did not have anything cooked. However, I did have some freshly baked pastries from a local French nouvelle brasserie in the closest town. I set the pastry basket in front of him. It was filled with vanilla and chocolate éclairs, flaky croissants, buttery brioche buns, and palmiers. Cam picked up a palmier and examined it like a biology project. He turned it upside down, right-side up, and upside down again.

"I don't even know how to eat this. Do I break or peel it?"

"No, goose, just bite it like a cookie. You like cookies, don't you?"

Cam picked up on what I was saying. He replied, "I love to eat cookies."

Robustly, Cam took a bite of the palmier. As he munched on it, he asked, "Why aren't you eating?"

"I can't. I'm watching my weight. Sig hates extra pounds. Plus I'm still in the running for the spokesmodel position."

"So you can't have any pleasure in your life, huh? Like these pastries. They taste so good, but you can only look at them. That is a sad way to live. Besides, you are already a remarkably beautiful woman—inside and out. Don't ever let anyone tell you otherwise."

I blushed. No one in my entire life had ever given me a sincere compliment. Sure, I have been told that I was pretty, beautiful even. But Cam's remark was not given to sway me into giving up parts of my integrity or soul. He was looking past my physicality and caught a glimpse of something more important. His admiration was given honestly and purely without any expectation of payback. I picked up a croissant and took a piece of it into my mouth. He smiled and clicked my croissant with the remainder of his palmier like we were clinking wine glasses.

After I poured both of us some coffee, Cam started probing me. "So what made you become a model anyway?" he asked, taking another bite of his palmier.

I took a sip of coffee, giving myself time to think about

an answer that would make me look good. However, I felt so relaxed by Cam's presence, I felt like telling the truth.

"Why modeling?" I said. "Well, I wasn't the brainiest, funniest, or most innovative in school. The one thing that I did receive praise for was my looks. So you have to exploit your best asset. My assets were my face and body. I meet a lot of people through my looks; that is how I survived. That's how I'm surviving now."

Cam pointed at my gourmet kitchen like it was nothing more than a ratted-out closet with a hotplate. "This is surviving? You live in a freak show. Sure, the tent is beautiful, but it is still a spectacle. I'm sorry to tell you, but you are not surviving. You are dying a slow death."

With those insightful words, Cam cut me to the quick. He said what I already knew but did not want to fully acknowledge. I was comfortable pretending everything was alright, that I was happy. If feelings to the contrary came up, I was a master at pushing them down. I knew that I could not allow myself to dwell upon the truth: that I was absolutely miserable. If I did that, I would have to take any and all responsibility for changing my lot. However, Cam had just called me out, and there was no way I could justify my actions.

It was time for some deflection. I said, "So what about you? Why did you become a lawyer? I mean it kind of seems like you are judging me for being aspirational. But the last time I checked, not many people become lawyers for the awesome chance to live in the poorhouse."

Whew! Good job, Lilly. Way to put Cam on the spot.

"Lilly, you don't understand. It isn't about the money. It's about the motivation. The reason *why* any of us do what we do," he responded.

"So in your mind, your motivation is better than mine."

Gotcha! Cam could not possibly come back from that line of reasoning. I relaxed confidently in my chair, relishing this chance to feel smug for a change. I could see him formulating a lawyer-like retort to throw back at me, and I could not wait to hear it. However, when Cam leaned in to deliver his argument, his gigantic hand knocked over his cup, spilling hot coffee right onto his jeans.

Wow! I actually made the great Cameron Sterling nervous. Was it my witty repartee? My deep observations? Did I sound like a Rhodes scholar?

When Cam sprung up from his chair, I knew it was not any of those things. It was something more basic: Cam's tree stump of a dick was rock hard. He just knocked over the cup because he was horny. I was disappointed for a few seconds. I actually allowed myself the thought that maybe he had been impressed by something special in me, something other than my body.

But then I had to admit something to myself. Up until that point, that was all that Cam was to me too—a scrumptiously delicious body. I could not be upset if he saw me as the same. Besides, that tempting snake in his jeans looked like it needed to be charmed.

I rushed over to Cam with a dishcloth and tried to vigorously rub the stain out of his jeans. As I stroked with urgency, I looked into his big, brown eyes. He had the same look that he had in the hallway during the gala—lusty. I could practically read his mind, and he was suggesting…no, demanding that I screw him right there on that kitchen table. I calculated in my mind how fast I could clear it: *Remove the pastries. Put the cups in the sink. Push the chairs back. Yeah, about fifteen seconds. And then it's time to fuck!*

Cam took me around the small of my waist. With an open mouth, he came at me. Just when things were about to go down, I heard someone clear their throat. Lin had come back into the kitchen. She was now a reluctant witness to a forbidden embrace and quickly lowered her head. I separated myself from Cam and tried to play it off the best I could.

"Lin, do you need something?" I asked her as I nervously tried to compose myself.

"The landscaper has cleared the leaves and needs your okay on the rest of the yard." Her head was still down; she was too embarrassed to look up.

I glanced back at Cam, who by that time had lost the stiffness of his manhood. I asked him, "Want to see the backyard?"

Cam took a hard look at my rounded behind. "Sure do."

After Lilly put on some warmer clothes, she and I stepped out of the black-framed French doors leading to the patio. Lilly went directly to the landscaper to give him an assessment of his work. While she was occupied with that, I turned my attention to the property.

From the elevated vantage point of the patio, the sight that greeted me was no ordinary backyard. I was looking over what could only be called a miniature kingdom.

I was rarely impressed by anything, but damn. It was as though God himself had painted a natural portrait on a canvas of air and made sure every color, shape, and sound was situated to duplicate heaven. This visual feast invited me to linger, take my time, and let it all soak in.

Acres and acres of property backed up to a wall of forest so dense it was the botanical equivalent of the Great Wall of China. A veritable field of grass that was as green as a praying mantis was cut with precision, all of its edges perfectly stiff and straight. Rock paths wound their way through massive gardens now dormant for the winter. What struck me as odd was a lonely Adirondack chair next to a fire pit. It had a flowered cushion, so I knew it was Lilly's. However, with Lilly and Sig sharing a house, really there should have been two chairs.

Another odd yet fascinating feature of the property was an enormous hedge maze. Its tall, evergreen shrubs formed a perfect square of what seemed to be infinite walkways. These wide passages did allow for some cut-throughs, yet I thought the entire maze was still too complicated of a fixture to be in someone's backyard. I wondered out loud, "Is the maze difficult to traverse?"

By this time Lilly had finished her business with the landscaper. Instead of answering me, she teasingly sprinted down the spiral steps tacked onto the side of the patio, toward the maze's entrance. She stood there for a moment just smiling at me with a catch-me-if-you-can look. Then she suddenly bolted into the maze. Of course I was not one to turn down a challenge and was immediately off to retrieve her. As I arrived at the fringe of the maze, I heard Lilly calling to me.

"Come and get me, Cam," she dared.

I like this playful Lilly.

Raising my eyebrow, I took up her taunting invitation. God help her when I caught her. Lilly's voice was growing softer, indicating that she was going deeper into the complex mesh of passages.

I was about to rush in, but nagging thoughts crept into my mind. Yes, I had decided that I was going to go with the flow and let whatever take its course. But that was ultimately submitting to the fickle whim of circumstance and relinquishing control of my own will. I already knew that I had given up a tremendous amount of control when Lilly answered the door. If I entered that maze, I could possibly be letting go of whatever control I had left. Fate and chance would have permission to step in and fuck me up.

"Lilly, I've delivered the papers. I should really be headed back to town," I yelled as I tried to regain my free will.

A distant voice blithely threatened me. "If you don't get in here right now, I am going to tell Sig that you did not want to cooperate with me. Then you'll be in big trouble."

Well, I could not disappoint the lady, now could I? That is the excuse I gave myself. I charged into the maze with every intention of capturing Lilly. But the maze proved to be more challenging than I thought. I decided to navigate it by only taking left-hand turns and following Lilly's giggly laughter. As I traversed the maze, I found myself actually having fun. The freezing temperature and extensive time I spent inside it did not bother me in the least.

I knew this game was just foreplay, and Lilly and I were building up heat. As I pursued her, I felt my already piqued desire growing beyond its normal boundaries. The excitement of the chase and anticipation of the reward of her body are what drove me down those endless paths in search of hidden pleasure.

Suddenly Lilly popped out of one of the shortcuts. She stood in front of me breathing hard, the cold vapor of her breaths shrouding her face like a veil. A wild surge of excitement rose in me at the mere sight of her. It was nearly impossible to stave off an impulse to throw her to the ground and make love to her ferociously. She gawked at me with wanton desire. Her moist, glossed lips eagerly waited for mine to engulf them.

But I did not kiss her. Instead I unzipped her coat. She had these tiny buttons on her pink blouse in the shape of flower petals. I started unbuttoning from the top, taking my time. I tested my limits with every button, but Lilly did nothing to stop me. Though my big fingers had trouble with the delicate buttons, I managed to open her shirt down to her navel. Her skin was flushed with desire and the burn of the numbing wind. I unclasped the front closure of her bra, and her round breasts burst forth. Her nipples, already hard before we even went outside, were now knotted up into two hard balls. I held one of her breasts in my hand. My tongue slowly and softly glided lightly over the nipple at first. Then I pursed my lips around it and suckled. Lilly grabbed the back of my head as I pushed her against the thick hedge.

I placed my other hand between her warm thighs, directly on her sweet spot. I caressed her through her pants. She was so excited that I could feel her body heat penetrate through the fabric. Lilly started to gyrate on my hand, dry humping it. I could not neglect the other breast, so I took it. I held it firmly, and this time I nibbled. I started gently and gradually increased the pressure. My bites were both stimulating and painful, filling her with a crazed thrill.

Just as Lilly reached for my jeans, a shrill and bothersome presence made itself known.

"Lilly! Where are you? You left the door wide open. And whose motorcycle is that?" screamed Sig from the patio.

Lilly looked scared shitless. The passion generating between us had been quelled. That cock-blocking Sig made sure of that. Lilly put her finger to her lips, telling me not to make a sound. Then she quickly buttoned up her shirt and whispered, "Sig can't know we're out here. Follow me."

Quickly, Lilly grabbed my hand, and we whisked through a shortcut in the maze. Once we were outside the shrubs, we ducked as we sneaked to the front of the house. I could see Sig standing on the patio like a dictator. He surveyed the maze, his instincts telling him Lilly was out there. I wanted to stand tall and let him know that I was with her. Just as I was about to show myself to Sig, Lilly looked back at me. Her face was so innocent, so naïve. She was dealing with this awkward situation the best she could. I did not want to cause her drama or harm, so despite my better judgment and pride, I relented and stayed crouched.

Finally, Lilly and I reached the front of the manse. She said, "Go to the living room. Pick up a book like you have been reading it the whole time."

She gave me a quick kiss. I was dumbstruck for a second at the sweet taste of her lips on mine. However, I recovered and entered the house right behind her. Lilly and I parted ways with her going upstairs and me going to the living room. I grabbed a hardbound book, a collector's copy of *The Scarlet Letter*. I flipped to some random page and waited.

This is some high-school bullshit. What am I doing? I should just tell Sig the truth. That I couldn't get Lilly off my mind. That I thought about her night and day. That I wanted to bed her.

But no matter how conflicted I was, I was not going to jeopardize Lilly's life. My selfish desires did not warrant the destruction of her well-crafted existence. And the main component of that existence—Sig—was now standing right behind me. I had actually smelled him before he entered the room. His repugnant odor was like a vile mix of bologna and seaweed.

"I did not see you when I came in. Where is Lilly?" Sig asked with more than a bit of suspicion.

I ran my finger over a line in the book, pretending like I was wrapping up a riveting paragraph. "I've been here the whole time. Lilly? I don't know. I think she's upstairs."

"Were you upstairs? Did you disrespect my house?"

"Like I told you, I have been here in the living room the whole time."

I hated lying. I prided myself on telling the truth all the time, no matter who it hurt. I did not even have to lie in my legal cases. Omission, yes. Lying, never. But today I made a concession for Lilly. However, Sig was not like the usual person on a jury. Sig was a feral animal like me. He had finely tuned instincts that had served him well. He knew bullshit when he heard it. Though he needed my expertise to pull off his legal case, I could tell that Sig and I would have to personally interface at some time.

Lilly came down the stairs as if nothing had happened. "Sig, I'm so glad you're home."

He pushed her away as she attempted to give him a hug. "Cam says that you were upstairs while he was down here." Sig studied Lilly's eyes. "Is that true?"

"Yes, yes. Why would you ask me such a thing?" She was a terrible liar. I knew I had to intervene before she outed both of us. I grabbed the paperwork and handed it to Sig, making sure I stood between him and Lilly.

"Mr. Kroc, Wotherspoon wanted me to deliver this to you personally. That is why I'm here. Nothing else."

Sig opened the envelope and started looking over the paperwork. His eyes opened wide with displeasure. Whatever was in that envelope surely did rattle him.

"Did you look at the contents?" Sig asked me. He was meeker in his tone now.

"No, I was just the deliverer. Why? Is there something I need to see?"

Sig quickly shoved the papers back into the envelope. "No, nothing. Cam, come with me to my office. Lilly, go back to whatever it is you do during the day."

All three of us left the living room together. Lilly and I passed each other a covert look before she disappeared into the house.

I followed Sig to his office. As we passed the kitchen, a terribly sour look drifted over Sig's face. Despite our best efforts to hide the romantic interlude we had earlier, Lilly and I had not covered all our tracks. Lin had not cleared the table yet, and Sig saw our two coffee cups.

He was on our scent now. But I could not blame him for being upset. Lilly was not my woman. She belonged to him. He was the one that had invested in her for whatever reason. Really, all Lilly and I had was an overpowering sexual attraction. I did not know her; she did not know me. I was the interloper, the intruder in his home. And I had indeed disrespected his house.

This situation reminded me that I had to get my head back on straight and remember my goal—making partner. It was a mistake to let down my guard like I had been doing. That is how people destroy themselves and others by neglecting to plan, use self-control, and take responsibility for outcomes. I should know. That is how it was when I was growing up. My mother did not take control of her situation and look what happened to her. She was now dead as fuck. I was not going to get caught like that. I had to get back in control. I would not let lust take me down.

Chapter Nine

It was evening by the time I got back to the city. Midtown was congested by a jumble of cars and trucks stuck during the rush-hour gridlock. It was times like those when I was glad to have a motorcycle. I was able to weave in and out of traffic, effortlessly passing slow or stopped vehicles and breezing between lanes. But my aggressive driving was not caused solely by a desire to efficiently move through traffic. It was because of what had happened later at Sig's house.

After I handed off the paperwork to Sig, there was really nothing left for us to talk about. It was strange being in the same room as him, knowing that I had almost fucked his woman a couple of times. And the way the pheromones permeated the air when Lilly and I were around each other, Sig could not help but pick up on what we had been doing. Moreover, I did not like having to sneak around. That was not who I was.

However, that is not what left me vexed. After Sig and I said our good-byes, Lilly joined us. She dutifully took up post next to her money, i.e., Sig. Sig then made it a point to grope her ass. Lilly responded to him with a playful smile. I could not tell whether or not it was an act, or if she truly enjoyed it. But what I did know is that I felt like a third wheel. It dawned on me that I still did not know this woman. The way she could go back and forth so effortlessly between two men was disconcerting.

Even though I felt a connection to Lilly, I was not going to be played. I gave her a polite good-bye and hopped on my bike. I had a sinking feeling all the way back to the city. I had never felt that before. I tried to discern exactly what it was. Then I figured it out. It was jealousy.

After that long ride I arrived at my building and felt something was off. I looked around. Nothing looked amiss. I walked up the stairs to my apartment but still could not shake that nagging feeling. Every few steps I would glance behind me, half expecting to be jumped. But nothing was lurking in the darkness—so it seemed.

I finally made it to my apartment's level and immediately trained my security camera toward the stairs. After a quick look-over, I let myself in. A figure from the dark jumped out. It tried to wrap itself around me but was so lightweight, I threw it off. I flipped on the light and was about to beat the shit out of that asshole. But what I saw sitting on my floor was no invader. It was Rebecca. No wonder I felt like I was being stalked.

"What in the flying fuck are you doing?" I yelled.

Rebecca still had her ass plastered to the floor and was propped up on her elbows. She was somewhat in shock. "What'd you do that for?"

I reached my hand out and helped her up. She rubbed her aching butt as my overzealousness had obviously hurt her. I created a wide distance between us by heading to the kitchen.

Rebecca said, "I know it's not Sunday night, but I thought I'd surprise you. Aren't you glad to see me?"

"I thought you were a burglar," I said, still walking away. I was pissed off that she was in my apartment. Fuck, how did she get into it in the first place? I swung around and asked her, "Rebecca, how did you get in here?"

Rebecca sauntered toward me. She had that dumb, pouty look on her face. "I told you to call me Becky. And to answer your question, I took the spare key. I didn't think you'd mind since I'm your girlfriend."

I did not take the time to correct her assertion. I was more interested in getting to my desk drawer, where I kept the spare key. Sure enough, it was gone. I looked at Rebecca. She was coyly swinging the key in front of her.

"Is this what you're looking for?"

"All right, enough playing around. Give me my key."

Rebecca shook her head no. "What are you so upset for? It's not like I'm a stranger. I practically live here. I am the girlfriend, right?"

"You don't live here, and you are not my girlfriend."

"We'll see about that."

Rebecca proceeded to strip off all her clothes. She did look hot thanks to a fresh spray-on tan and hours of kickboxing. She was vibrant, so very much alive as juxtaposed to my current depressed state. She put her finger in her mouth, sucked, and pulled it out. She then ran her wet fingertip over my lips.

"I'm sorry. Do you forgive me, Daddy?"

The "Daddy" part threw me for a loop, but that did not stop my dick from getting hard. I felt her hand softly grope my balls, using her finger to stroke and separate them. She drew in closer to me and stood on her toes so she could kiss my neck. I tried not to let her get to me, but I gave in to her seductive truce. I found myself putting my arms around her and kissing her back.

I had no love for Rebecca, but I was man. I did man shit. And an integral part of man shit is fucking a woman who is just basically putting her pussy out there. Plus I was still hot and bothered from the interrupted sexcapade between Lilly and me.

Besides, I was a free agent. It was not like Lilly and I had some sort of real relationship. We just *almost* fucked a lot. And based on the way that Sig was fondling her ass today, Lilly was probably getting the shit fucked out of her at that very moment. In fact, it was only logical that Sig was fucking her. No rational man "keeps" a woman without fucking her.

So it made no sense to pass up sex with Rebecca—someone I had been fucking all along. Also I just wanted to feel better, to get out of this stupid funk.

With a clear conscious I decided to indulge myself with Rebecca. She wasted no time undressing me. Hell, she was so ravenous that I thought she was going to rip the buttons off my shirt and the zipper out of my jeans. Rebecca positioned herself on the floor and then spread her legs. Her juices were plentiful, glistening, and thick. In a fell swoop I mounted her. As I inserted my thick knob deeper inside, I heard her gasping for breath as ecstasy overtook her.

Though my body was there with Rebecca, my mind was still on Lilly. I looked down and superimposed Lilly's face onto hers. My dick seemed to grow even longer, and my pelvis started to pound into Rebecca's with more vigor. The more I thought about Lilly, the faster I pumped. Rebecca called out my name as she came hard. I came, too, and had to stifle the urge to scream Lilly's name.

Rebecca tried to keep me on top of her in an effort to bond. But I rolled off of her as fast as I could. Still breathing hard, she looked over at me with utter amazement. "Damn, what got into you? That was the best sex I ever had. Jesus, did you take vitamins today or what?"

I just lay there quietly as Lilly drifted from my mind like a ghost.

Rebecca put her hand on my stomach and grinned at me. "I can stay tonight. You know, pretend like we're married…Mr. and Mrs. Sterling. I can even make you some dinner. What do you want? Steak? Chicken? More of me?"

I gave her a sideways glance. "Not hungry. Had croissants."

Rebecca rose up and looked at me like I was a stranger to her. "Croissants?" she said incredulously. "Since when do you eat croissants? That is in no way your style."

"Yeah, croissants," I responded. I stood up and put my underwear back on. I pointed at Rebecca's bra. "Make sure you don't forget that. That way, you don't have to come back for it."

"You could give me a drawer, and I can leave it in there."

"Nah, I don't have any extra space. Where is your car parked? I have—"

Rebecca finished my thought for me. "I know. You're tired and have to get up early in the morning. I know the routine."

I actually felt sorry for her. She sounded so pitiful and was genuinely hurt. She was trying so hard to be a girlfriend. The problem was that she was dealing with a man who did not want to be her boyfriend. In some ways, it was my fault. I was leading her on, making her live in some sort of limbo. What I perceived to be a clearly designated hookup relationship, she saw as a real pairing. I was not trying to give mixed signals, but apparently I had.

For once I showed Rebecca some compassion. After we got dressed, I escorted her to her car. I had never done that before.

She looked up at me as if pleading for me to love her. Then I did something else that I had never done before—hugged her. Not out of affection but sympathy, like she was a wounded animal. Really, I was not a sadist; I did not get off on causing pain to another.

Rebecca clung to me. "Cam, I love you. All I ever wanted was for you to love me back. Tell me I'm not wrong for that… please."

I had to push her away so that she would release me. I did not want to devastate her with the truth, not that night anyway. I already had my own emotional issues to deal with. So I did the best I knew to do. I kissed Rebecca on her forehead and made sure she was secure in her car. She turned on the engine and let the window down. I spoke to her as though she were a child. I also made sure not to lean into the window, avoiding the chance that she would kiss me. "Let me know you got home safe," I said.

Unfortunately, Rebecca took my words as a sign of love. She perked up and said, "Okay, I will. As soon as I get home." She paused for a moment then continued, "You know, you can come over to my place sometime. I already have a drawer waiting for you."

That made me cringe. I stepped away from the car as I waved Rebecca off. With renewed hope, she disappeared into the evening darkness.

Chapter Ten

I started my day with an early morning run at The Equity. I told myself that I was only there to clear my head. But I knew that in the back of my mind, I was really there on the off-chance that I would run into Lilly.

The hours slowly ticked by, indicated by the large clock hanging ominously on the stark white wall. According to my treadmill, I had run ten miles. However, I was so focused on the door, hoping Lilly would come through it, that I did not even notice how far I had run. I had to get away from that clock. I went over to some weights situated near a line of windows. I tried not to look out of them, but I could not help scouring the street below hoping to catch sight of Lilly.

In an effort to stave off the desire to see her, I added more weight to the barbell. With every repetition, my restlessness grew. I moved on to a boot camp class already in progress. Nothing I did could burn up the excess energy in me. And Lilly was still nowhere to be seen. Despite the multiple workouts I had, I still considered the visit to be a bust. The only other thing I could think to do was go to the office. I took my time packing my gear. Still no Lilly.

Shit. Just get over it. She is not coming. She is at home probably not even thinking about you. Why are you wasting time on this woman? Focus on work. Get that promotion.

I followed my own advice and went straight to work. Since it was the weekend, and no one else was there, I did not see the need to take a shower and relished my own naturalness.

When I entered my office, I discovered that someone had put a folder on my desk. I opened it and saw it was filled with more of Sig's financial records. He had been a bad boy indeed. Lucky for him, he had beaucoup money and people like me who knew how to hide assets and monies for him. If Sig had been a regular, blue-collar guy, the IRS would have thrown him in prison a long time ago.

One thing for sure was that whoever the mysterious Z was, Sig had been shelling out big bucks. Even though the purchases were listed as business expenditures, I could tell that they were in essence gifts. A house in Thailand. Cars. Monthly food allowances. These "expenditures" had added up to roughly two million dollars. I could have pestered the partners to reveal to me more about who this Z person was. But ultimately my only job was just to make the numbers appear to be legit, and I was good at that.

There was something else in the folder—a Blu-ray disc. I scooted my chair over to the disc player that I used when studying footage of depositions. As the video streamed across the television screen, I realized that it was from the gala. Wotherspoon and Associates had a habit of secretly taping everything they were involved in. I did not even know who filmed this.

I fast-forwarded to the part where Lilly first entered the ballroom. When her winsome face filled the screen, my terrible longing for her grew with a vengeance. I was helpless to stop it. With almost unbearable yearning, I kept watching until the disc reached the part where Lilly was being interviewed. I pushed pause on the remote, and Lilly's image froze. The most primal part of my being wanted to set off back to Sig's house and bring Lilly back home with me. But if I did that, all hell would break loose. I would be fired and disbarred more than likely. Lilly would lose any shot at her dream of becoming the face of Klå, and it would be doubtful she could ever secure any other work as a model. We would be two pathetic souls, not to mention broke. But the sex would be wild.

No, passion was not reason enough to put Lilly through a living hell. All this back and forth was making me crazy anyhow. For now it was best to keep some space between Lilly and me until cooler heads and genitals could prevail.

〰〰

I found myself pacing back and forth in front of Klå head-quarters. The building was located only a block away from Central Park. It was nothing to see a celebrity out for a morning jog or walking their children to some exclusive private school. But lately I was shocked by the number of these famous people who actually knew who I was for a change. This was all because of Sig's prodigious reputation. As his girlfriend, I gleaned some of that mystique by proxy. Everyone was so fascinated that I actually made Sig settle down into what falsely appeared to be domestic bliss.

But if there had been any real bliss to it, I would not have been standing there. Though I kept my head down to keep from being recognized, I was still being inundated by never-ending hellos from longtime employees cycling in and out.

I tried to be polite and look as nonsuspect as possible. But I could see that a few of them were not falling for my bad acting job and wondered why in the hell I was shuffling outside the building like I was homeless. Little did they know that a crazy internal debate was oscillating inside of me.

See, the memory of Cam's sizzling touch was still scorching my skin. That was a huge problem for me because now a sexual combustion inflamed me, and I had not been able to put it out. I did not even have his phone number or an email address, which was so silly to me considering that I let that man suck my nipples.

I was pushed by my libido to get in contact with Cam. Practically all of my waking hours for the past couple of days revolved around trying to get that information. That Cam, he was a mysterious one. He had made sure that none of his personal information was out there. No Facebook. Twitter. Shit, not even Pinterest. Even if I did have his contact information, I would not have had a legitimate reason for contacting him.

But fuck it. I was horny, and my body was in desperate need of satisfaction. Yes, I could have had the usual mechanical-style coitus with Sig. However, all that would have done was piss me off and drive me closer to sticking a fork in his eye. I wanted Cam. He was the only one who could satisfy me.

A disturbing thought stopped in my tracks right in the middle of the sidewalk. *Could I actually be addicted to Cameron Sterling?*

I examined the evidence. I had absolutely no control over the frenetic thoughts about Cam that constantly bombarded me. I had felt ridiculously jittery and moody ever since our romp in the maze. In fact my psychological tension had ratcheted up until it hit such a painful denouement that it could only be compared to a panic attack. That is why I was compelled by a seemingly unnatural force to get into my car and drive like a mindless zombie to New York. Yeah, I was definitely obsessed.

Now I found myself pacing and shivering outside a warm building next to a hoarded-up group of smokers. They were willing to brave icy conditions just to get a nicotine fix. I, however, had a different fix in mind. Like with any drug, I was past merely wanting Cam; I needed him. So as far as addiction symptoms went, I scrolled down my list and checked off every one. Right then I finally came to terms about my feelings for Cam and what the unpleasant consequences could mean for me. I did not care anymore; I was willing to risk them.

Despite my decision to be a philanderer, I felt no guilt, quite the contrary. A sense of calm cascaded over me as I went from ambiguous to steadfast with the goal of procuring Cam's phone number and address. The problem was how I could do it without arousing the suspicion of Klå's loyal and gossipy employees. I decided to just go for it as I strolled into the building's atrium.

Those uninitiated into the gratuitous lifestyle of the rich were always gobsmacked into a stupor when they entered its fabled doors. Sig made sure no expense was spared when it came to designing Klå headquarters. The entrance consisted of an abnormally tall revolving door with burnished trim. Each of its four panels displayed the Klå trademark—a red cross with a thorny rose. One of the first things that greeted you as you exited the roundabout was the intoxicating scent. The dreamy aroma was like a finger that dragged you around by the nose.

It was a clean yet decidedly masculine smell that reminded me of a day at the beach. It was piped through the vents and was thick enough to replace the oxygen.

Going deeper, the magnificent atrium would make Prince Alwaleed drop to his knees in awe. It was so massive I might as well have entered inner earth. I needed sunglasses to protect my eyes from the gleam of the highly glossed stone floors with glittery flecks for more luminous effect. Large planters and gigantic indoor trees gave the illusion of being in a tropical rainforest. All the plants stretched toward the high ceiling as if reaching for heaven. Back on earthly ground, a crush of unblemished models carried look books, while aspiring fashion designers towed sketches and fabric swatches.

My attention gravitated toward the models the most. They scared me. Though I was a model, there was never a point in my career when I had any of the confidence that those ladies and gentlemen had. The only way I could fake it was when I sneaked a few tranquilizers and liquor. I could not dwell on that too much, though. I was on a mission.

Somewhere between the sidewalk and the atrium, things started to change. Sure, when I first entered Klå's doors, I was full of myself and basically beating my chest. With the thought of Cam driving me, I felt like I could change the rotation of the planet. Confidence crackled out of me like electricity. However, my hubris was short-lived. With every step the shadow of my insecurity popped me on the back of the head, reminding me of my utter nothingness. Really, who did I think I was fooling, trying to play a secret agent gathering information from behind enemy lines?

I eventually made it to the corporate office's main floor and was somewhat relieved that Katie Bean, one of Sig's secretaries, was working that day. Katie was an older lady who had youthful dreams of being a designer in the industry, but they never came to fruition. She took on whatever industry-related job she could, always hoping to catch a break. But age had caught up to her, and now all she could do was work behind a desk at Klå. She was reconciled to her fate and had come to accept this opportunity. It gave her a chance to have a reason to dress stylish every day and kept her young at heart. Today Katie looked exceptionally sexy for a woman in her sixties, dressed in a tight pencil skirt and high-heeled Mary Janes.

Though I liked Katie, I was terrified of becoming her. Her life was the embodiment of that poem "A Dream Deferred." I did not want to have a life of unfulfilled goals and settling for the next best thing. As I made my way toward Katie, I glanced up at effigies of former Klå spokesmodel superstars. My feet got heavy, and I started to move like I was trudging through sludge. Those images seemed to look down on me, judging and laughing. Like they knew I would never be one of them.

Regroup, Lilly. No time to think about becoming the face of Klå. Cam is what you are after now.

With Cam being my guiding light, I gained some mental hysterical strength and was able to continue with my quest. With steady confidence, I fended off my anxiety and managed to smile.

"Good morning, Ms. Amsel," Katie said, beaming. "What can I do for you today?"

Okay. Look Katie straight in the eye, flash her a smile, and lie your ass off.

I said, "Actually, you can do a lot for me. See, Sig is meeting an important client today, but I really need to get in contact with him."

Katie went through Sig's appointment book. "I don't see a meeting scheduled for Sig today. Just a spa day."

Great. Katie's on to me. Never mind that. Just keep on lying.

I whispered, "It's a secret meeting. You know, all that legal stuff with Wotherspoon. But I really need to talk to him, and he's not picking up his phone. He never does when he is in those types of meetings. But I think I know who he's meeting up with. Um, I think his name is Cameron Sterling. I know that Klå has a database of client numbers. Could you look up Mr. Sterling's number for me? I'd greatly appreciate it."

I tapped my foot nervously, knowing she would not believe that cockamamie story. However, I had some good karma built up. Katie looked around, making sure no one was watching us. "Normally I would not do this. But seeing that you are Sig's girlfriend, and you have been so very nice to me in the past, I'll do this favor for you. Just please don't tell Sig I gave it to you."

Katie got right on her computer and pulled Cam's information. She wrote down not only his phone number but his business and home addresses. Talk about a stroke of luck.

Little did I know that as I was sneaking information about Cam, someone was watching me—Jacob. He lurked just beyond our view and had been observing everything. His fiendish eyes narrowed as he plotted against me.

I thanked Katie and left as quickly as I could before I fumbled my fib. As soon as I got into the elevator, Jacob crept over to Katie. He did not waste a moment interrogating her. "I see that Lilly came by. What's going on with her?" he asked in a lispy voice.

Katie's subconscious read Jacob. Having worked with Sig's simultaneously bipolar and withdrawn personality, she knew a tricky person when she saw one. However, at his young age,

Jacob had not mastered the art of controlling body language to conceal his true motives. He was rigid and was motioning like he was choking an invisible person. Also, with offhand antipathy, Jacob was looking at Katie like a sadistic child readying himself to pull the wings off a butterfly.

"Ms. Amsel? It was personal," Katie said as she immediately closed out the window on her computer. "Don't you have some fittings today? I would hate for you to miss those."

But Katie did not close the computer before Jacob read the phone number. He was somewhat of a savant. His Asperger's syndrome gave him the gift of an eidetic memory when it came to number sequences.

"Oh, Katie. I'm in no hurry to be fitted. I'd rather be here with you, enjoying this conversation," Jacob said, not letting on that he got the digits.

Katie's hairs rose like a flag on the back of her neck. Jacob's pinpoint pupils were dead set on her. He leaned into her personal space, and Katie went right into his. For a few moments no words were exchanged, just a weird psychic standoff. But Jacob had not counted on age winning before ruthlessness and reluctantly relented, knowing that Katie was not going to back down.

"Alright then. I guess I will go to my fitting." But before he got on the elevator, he turned back to Katie. "Be careful around here. You never know who is gunning for you."

Jacob got on the elevator and promptly pulled out his cell phone. He went to the Internet and did a reverse number lookup. Nothing came up.

"That's okay," Jacob said to himself. "I'm going to destroy Lilly one way or the other."

Chapter Eleven

I was so relieved when Tamara called to invite me to lunch. It gave me a reason to delay calling Cam.

Tamara let me pick the spot. I am sure she was expecting me to choose some swank restaurant. But I decided to cheat on my diet and get a greasy burger and onion rings from a hole in the wall instead. The restaurant did not have a formal name, just a sign that said "burgers." I used to eat there when I first came to New York and was beyond broke. The restaurant was small and could only fit three tables. The utilitarian atmosphere was abetted by the peeled lime-green vinyl chairs and an old-fashioned soda fountain. The Middle Eastern immigrants who ran it made no ado about the interior decoration. They made up for it with the food.

After a brief wait, the ruddy owner yelled out that our order was ready in a tongue I did not know, his hand furiously waving us over. Tamara paid, though not impressed at all by what she saw. As the food was handed to us in brown paper bags, I could see her about to upchuck. She was fully focused on the grease soaking through and almost looked like she wanted to cry. The grease did not matter to me, even though I knew it would be on my thighs the next morning.

I enthusiastically sat down, while Tamara wiped off her seat. She gave me a look and sat down. Tamara was not expecting what happened next. She opened her bag, and a whiff of that glorious burger hit her nose—that aroma of perfectly charred beef. She started looking at the burger like it was a guy she should not want to fuck but really wanted to.

"Are you sure we should be eating this?" she asked, secretly admiring the melty cheese nestled under a pile of freshly cut vegetables and a colorful array of condiments.

I laughed because I knew where all this food angst was coming from. Tamara, having grown up in an upper-class community in her native Trinidad, was a bit of a food snob. She found it nearly impossible to enjoy the fare of regular folks. I, on the other hand, grew up in a trailer park, and this was good eating to me. I watched with amusement as she smooshed her face and pulled back her locs as not to contaminate them with an accidental brush with the ketchup.

"Tam, stop fooling around and just taste it," I said. I then took a big bite, encouraging her to do the same. As both of us bit down through the layers of flavor, we simultaneously had food-gasms. Though my eyes instinctive rolled back, Tamara had an even more profound reaction. She moaned and gripped the table with her free hand. Then she started tapping the table rhythmically with her fingertips as the burger made her hear music. As Tamara slipped down into the chair, coupled with the thick grease dripping down the sides of her mouth, she looked almost like she was having a seizure.

"Whew! Goddamn, that was good," she said, basking in a burger-induced afterglow.

I knew how she felt. That's how Cam made me feel every time I was with him. God, I really wanted to call him. I should have memorized his telephone number because I didn't want Sig to know I had it. But I didn't trust myself not to freeze up and forget it. I just had to make sure my cell phone was password locked. I had come so close to calling him several times but always lost my nerve.

I had to get some advice, so I just blurted out, "I'm fooling around on Sig."

Tamara nearly shit her pants and blew her burger out of her mouth. "What the hell did you just say?"

"I'm dicking around. Well, not technically dicking. We haven't had real sex yet."

"I don't want to hear this. I'm not an accessory to your shenanigans," Tamara said, covering her ears.

"Please, I need some advice. I don't know what to do. I think I'm in love."

"And you are also very much in a relationship with Sig Krok, who happens to not only be your boyfriend but your livelihood too. Who is this other man anyway?"

"You saw him at the gala. The attorney."

"The sexy one with the chocolate eyes."

I blushed. "Yeah, that one."

Tamara took a breath. "I can see your dilemma. That man certainly is a tasty morsel. So I guess you want me to give you permission to call him and make a date. Run off and fuck him. Live happily ever after, right?"

"Pretty much."

"Well, missy, I'm not going to tell you what to do. But I will advise you to do whatever will make your heart smile."

With that, I dialed Cam's number. As the phone rang, my heart tried to beat its way out of my chest. I mentally searched for an excuse for calling him. Nothing came to mind. I decided to just wing it. The phone went to voicemail. Cam's voice was so deep, resonant, and smooth. It was like he had made that message just for seducing me. It worked. I wanted to see him even more.

"I've got to go," I said as I put on my coat.

"Where are you going?" asked Tamara.

"This may sound crazy as hell, but I'm going to his place. I just have to see him."

"You are playing with fire, you know."

Tamara was right. I was playing a dangerous game, and if Sig caught me, that would be my ass. Sig had the money and connections to really mess me up. But something out of my control was propelling me toward Cam. There was no stopping me.

———

I arrived at what appeared to be an abandoned warehouse. I double checked the address that Katie had given me. Sure enough, it matched.

A piece of masking tape was positioned over an intercom button. It had a short, handwritten message on it—"press me"—in permanent marker. I did as instructed, half expecting the bell not to work. I listened hard for a chime or any type of ring coming from inside the huge building. There was just silence. I was getting ready to walk away when I heard a dis-embodied voice.

"Yes?" Cam said. His tone was perplexed, somewhat suspi-cious. I could tell he did not receive many visitors. His voice, no matter how uptight it sounded, made my hormones flow like hot lava. For a moment I was dumbstruck. I could not say a word. Hearing his voice just did me in.

Cam came back over the intercom, more irritated this time. "Hello. Who is it?"

I took a brave breath, and a squeaky utterance came out of me. "Uh, Cam. This is Lilly. Lilly Amsel."

After what seemed like an eternity of uncomfortable silence, he said, "Take the elevator."

I heard the automatic buzz of the door as it was opened for me then stepped into a cavernous space. It was a welcome surprise from the exterior. Someone had put a lot of effort into converting the area. Yet there was still something about it that made it feel hollow and lifeless. I stepped onto the elevator and ascended to the upper level.

Suddenly I felt so foolish—stalkerish—for being at Cam's home. I needed a valid excuse to be there, something other than getting my freak on. I decided to say that I was there to apologize for what happened in the maze and that I had no intentions to harm his career in any way. I checked my reflection on the elevator's shiny wall and adjusted my tits so they popped out just right.

As soon as the doors opened, I saw Cam was standing there. Of course he was looking delicious as usual. He was dressed very dapper in an all-black suit, and his dark hair was gelled down, black as an oil slick. I was getting ready to give him my spiel about our tryst in the maze and my fake apology, but he spoke first.

"I'm really glad to see you." He did not look like he was happy to see me at all. A cloud of melancholy hovered over him. Cam tried to give me a gloomy smile but just could not muster it. He took my hand and led me into his apartment. It was minimalist in its furnishings and manly in its taste but felt just as empty as the rest of the building.

Cam was quiet. He looked at me with sorrow. My own insecurity immediately took it personally, making me think I had done something to offend him.

"What's wrong, Cam? Did I come at a bad time? I mean I did show up unannounced."

He took a deep breath. The air came out of him as if his breath had barbed wire in it.

"It's not you. I've got to go to this today." He handed me an invitation for a memorial service. It was for Luisa Maria Fontenelli Sterling…Cam's mother, who died twenty years ago.

Way to go, Lilly. You are officially a piece of shit. Coming over here strictly to get fucked, while this man is dealing with some heavy crap.

I tried to make amends. "And here I am bothering you. I am so sorry. I'll leave."

"No, I'm actually glad you're here."

Cam pulled me close to his body. I could tell by the way he embraced me that he was drawing from my life force. I hugged him back and allowed him to feed on my essence as much as he could.

"Who are you going with? Friends? Family?" I asked.

Cam let me go. "No one. I have no one."

I knew him well enough to know that normally he would tout that as a point of pride. It showed that he did not need anyone to complete or support him. But today he sounded like he had some regret over being such a loner.

"You don't have to worry about that. No one should have to be alone at a time like this. I'll go with you," I said, stroking his chin. Cam smiled as an inkling of relief entered his mind.

Then he kissed me. It was a short kiss and ever so delicate. Yet it was one of the sweetest kisses I had ever known.

I didn't mind driving Cam to the memorial service. We did not speak along the way. He mostly looked out the window. Whenever I could catch a glimpse of his face, I could see that he had been transported back in time to when his mother was alive. When an occasional smile would cross his face, he was thinking of a happy time. Sometimes his brow would scrunch and his lips would curl as he remembered something awful. I wanted to ask him so badly what was going on in his head, but it was not appropriate.

We arrived at Mayflower Memorial Gardens. It was a terribly depressing place. The winter had set the sun behind a near-permanent gray veil of sky. The bare trees and brown grass were the perfect accompaniment to all the death surrounding us.

A winding gravel road led us past endless rows of the headstones marking snuffed-out lives. We passed a funeral in progress. A young boy stood near the coffin of his mother as his father held his hand. The boy expressed no emotion like he had totally disconnected from reality. Cam looked away from the child. I could see the genesis of his aloof personality.

Luisa was buried at the back of the cemetery. I was expecting to see a crowd of people. But as we pulled up, I just saw a pastor and an elderly woman. The old woman turned around when she heard my car and immediately zeroed in on the passenger seat. Her face lit up as she recognized Cam, and though she was disabled, she sprinted over to us the best she could.

Without even thinking, the old woman opened Cam's door and dragged him out. She grabbed him and hugged him like she were his own mother. As I got out of the car, I could see that Cam was overwhelmed by her enthusiastic response, but he relaxed and went with it.

"Cam, it has been so long, too long, since I've seen you. Look at you. You've grown up into such a good-looking man. Luisa would've been so proud."

I felt a bit awkward, like a third wheel. I did not know exactly what to do except to stand next to Cam. I smiled awkwardly as the elderly woman finally paid attention to me.

"Is this your girlfriend?"

Cam did not deny me. Instead, he said, "This is Lilly. Lilly, this is Hilda Brown. Ms. Brown was my neighbor when I was a little boy. She and my mother were best friends."

I held my hand out toward Ms. Brown, but she took me in a tight bear hug instead. "Oh, call me Hilda. It's so nice to know that Cam found such a nice girl. I bet you are the one who convinced him to come out here."

"No, ma'am. He invited me," I responded as she released me.

"I've had a hard time getting him to come to one of these memorials," said Hilda as she led Cam and me to Luisa's grave. From the condition of the headstone, it was obvious that no one had visited for a while. Cam could not look at it. His eyes went to the trees, the road, to me, and anything else that would prevent him from looking directly at the grave.

The pastor observed Cam's discomfort and was kind enough to get the memorial started so it could be over quickly. His beautiful service lasted about twenty minutes. It ended with Cam putting the roses on the headstone. He kneeled down and touched it. I could see a tiny tear forming in the corner of his eye.

Hilda pulled me aside to let Cam have some time alone with his mother and to have a word with me. "I was really worried about Cam the past years. Even though he had a rough start, he was still a happy little boy. After his mother passed away, though, he was never the same. When she died, some of him died with her."

"What happened? Cancer? Accident?" I asked.

"Oh, child. He didn't tell you? His father killed her when he was five. A murder-suicide right in front of him. His father was an atrocious man—a drunkard who beat Luisa mercilessly. I begged her to leave him, and I even called the cops a few times. But she loved him and did not want to break up the family. Old-school Catholic she was."

I looked back at Cam, who was now giving the pastor a hefty tip. At that moment I did not see Cam the grown man but the injured child that was left behind. Cam and I had much more in common than I could have imagined.

Hilda said, "After Cam's mother died, I wanted to take him in. But with me being so poor and having six children of my own, I just couldn't do it. He wound up in foster care. I kept up with him the best I could and learned that he developed some behavior problems. No one likes problem children, so he was bounced around every few months. Sometimes they handled him with violence."

"But things got better, right?" I asked.

"That boy always had a plan. Cam somehow still managed to keep his grades up and become a stellar athlete. He even became an all-American. I contacted him around that time when I had the first memorial for Luisa. He didn't show up. He was so young and still had not dealt with losing Luisa. Years passed, and I lost touch. The twenty-year anniversary of

Luisa's death came up, and I located Cam again. I was so happy to hear he had accomplished so much. And on top of that he found love."

Even though Cam had not corrected Hilda about the nature of our relationship, I felt it was necessary that this kind woman knew the truth. "I'm not his girlfriend. I'm just a friend."

Hilda flashed me a wide grin. "Darling, the way Cam looks at you, I can tell that whatever you guys have runs much deeper than friendship."

Chapter Twelve

I accompanied Cam back to his apartment after the memorial service. Despite my concerned protest, he decided that he wanted to drive back home. I knew this was an effort to keep his mind occupied and off the service.

"Thanks for going with me. You didn't have to do that. That was very kind of you," Cam said as he put his warm hand on my knee. I was not some sociopath who did not grasp the grave emotional atmosphere in the car. I was not a totally selfish cow either. However, I could not help that a ball of fire erupted in me that was ignited by Cam's touch.

"No problem. Anybody would've done it," I said, trying not to let my voice quiver. I glanced over at Cam, who by now had put on his shades. He was so ridiculously hot right then. No matter how he might have felt, he looked so calm and confident. He loosened his shirt and tie, ensuring a beguiling casualness that drew me in even more. Then he slightly slouched down into the driver's seat and leaned in toward me. I reciprocated by coyly pressing my small shoulder against his rippled upper arm. As Cam nuzzled closer to me, my eyes drew up to his face, where I could see that his five-o'clock shadow was beginning to sprout along his chiseled jawline. A hint of a rustic mountain man was breaking out of his cosmopolitan shell.

I tilted my head onto his arm. Keeping his eyes on the

road, Cam inhaled the scent of my hair. He said, "You smell so good right now."

I blushed as I reveled in his compliment. I was delighted, thrilled, to be in that car with Cameron. I wished it were under different circumstances. But I was taking what I could get. For the duration of the drive, I could pretend…pretend that Cam was my man, and I was his woman. Pretend that all was right in the world. No Sig. No Jacob. No thoughts about my past. I felt free.

After a nearly trafficless drive, we finally arrived back at Cam's place. We both sat in the car silently pondering what to do next. I figured I had overstayed my welcome.

"Well, I guess I should go home," I said as I opened the car door a tad.

"No. I want you to stay. For once I don't want to be alone."

Cam used his finger to softly put my hair behind my ear. His eyes seared into me, and I melted into the seat. I could tell that not only did he want me there; he needed me there. Never in my life had anyone needed me. That was different for me because I always needed everyone else. It felt good to be the one needed for a change. Because Cam trusted me, I could not abandon him. I said, "Okay, I'll stay. For you. I'll stay."

***

I was concerned about Cam. He looked fine in the car, almost as though the memorial service had not even fazed him.

But as we entered his apartment, I noticed he became more self-contained. As an expert in emotional suppression, I could always tell when someone else was doing it. I knew he was struggling with all that caged-in despair. The sweet thing was that Cam was holding his pain down for me. He was trying to make me feel comfortable and wanted me to feel good. He took no account of his own hurt, which lay just under his skin. Yet I could still feel his pain radiating out of him…achy, like he had the flu.

Cam did not even have the momentum to plop down in his favorite chair. Like a beat-up athlete, he slowly lowered himself into it. He eased back and put his hands up to his eyes. I could tell that he did not know how to rid himself of the pain of losing his mother or the rage he felt toward his father for taking her away.

I had to do something. There was no way I could erase the past and bring his mother back. I could only please him with whatever was immediately available. "Babe, you just sit there and relax. I'm going to make you a nice cup of tea."

Cam reached his hand out to me and gave me a sullen smile. I know it was wrong, but I could not help that his touch caused a thousand tiny fires to burn inside of me.

"You know my mother used to make me tea when I was sick. That is one of the things I miss about her the most."

I gave Cam a wink as his fingers unlocked from mine.

"Be right back," I said as I made my way to the kitchen.

"Could you put some rum in it?"

"Sure thing."

When I entered the kitchen, from that angle I could still see Cam. I could tell that his brain was projecting a movie about the day his mother died. I found myself entering his nightmare with my own imaginings. I saw random images of Cam's mother pleading for his father not to hurt him. Others images showed the glint of his father's revolver, first pointed at Cam and then his mom. The last part of the shared mental movie was vivid and much too raw, like lemon juice on an open cut. It was the bang of the gun.

The whistle of the teakettle jolted me back to reality. I then entered the den with Earl Grey tea swirled with a bit of cream and heavily spiked with rum. I could see that Cam had been railing against his melancholia, as indicated by the faint layer of sweat on his brow. I put the tea down and squatted between his legs. He pulled forward as he wrapped his masculine arms around my lower back. The ridges of his rock-hard abs pressed against me. His rough hands rubbed up and down my sides as he brought me closer to his engorged cock. I was a mess inside and did not know how to deal with the lascivious charge ricocheting inside me.

Was this appropriate at that moment? I mean I was there to help him. But things were somehow turning around. I realized that I wanted relief too. Cam was intuitive enough to pick up on it. He put his lips just below my ear. I relished the warmth of his breath on my skin.

Cam said, "You and me, we have a lot in common. I don't know that much about you, but I can see that you are broken like me, a wounded person. I know old wounds that cut deep never really fade. Inside scars aren't pretty. See, people like us just want to cut off the heads of the demons in our past. If we don't, grief will snuff us out. I don't have control over every-thing, but I can control this: I want to make you feel better. I *have* to make you feel better, and I will so that we can both be free. So tonight we have a choice. Either we can continue living in misery with our very souls slipping away, or we can liberate each other."

"Let the liberating begin," I said.

I then felt Cam's plump, wet lips on mine. He kissed my lips slowly as if they were virgins he was about to deflower. Next thing I knew, he was nibbling them. His bites got progressively harder, so primal, as he was driven by his pain and desire for my deliverance.

"Lilly, I want to make love to you," Cam breathily said.

He did not let me give him any sort of response. Instead he swept me up with desperate urgency. I wrapped my long, slender legs around his waist as he took me to bed. Hell, I was practically perched on top of his enormous dick. With every step, it rubbed my clit perfectly. Though I still had under-wear on, my lips had engorged enough to where they almost wrapped around his shaft.

With all barriers collapsing between Cam and me, our bodies fused as they wantonly expressed our total vulner-ability and honesty. All I wanted was for Cam to thrust hard and become one with me. Our tongues came together like two vipers intertwining. Cam took the lead and sucked my tongue almost right out of my head. I could feel the power and strength behind his tongue. He took, and I gave. Mmm, he tasted divine with hints of tea, cream, and rum still lingering on his tongue.

With no consideration for delicacy, Cam tossed me on the bed. For just the tiniest of moments, we just stared at each other for a while, trying to capture in memory our lives before we passed over the crossroad, the termination of our old existences. I then stood on my knees and pulled my sweater over my head. Wispy strands of my hair landed over my eye.

I watched Cam as he watched me, his gaze penetrating all the way to my anguished soul. Finally, here was a man who could truly know, understand, and accept me.

Cam undressed me without even consciously thinking about it. And that was a good thing because I was absolutely hypnotized by him.

Fuck! I'm acting like I'm comatose. Okay, Cam didn't slip me a roofie, nor have I been lobotomized. Wake up, bitch. Wake up.

"Don't worry, baby. I got this," Cam said as he started unzipping my ankle-skimming skirt. I assisted him by sitting on my hip so that I could get out of my clothes faster. In one cocksure move, Cam removed not only my skirt but my panties too.

"I was half expecting to see some racy red lace hiding under your clothes. But it's sexy as fuck that you were wearing a simple cotton bikini." He then examined my undies more closely.

"My God, with tiny cherries on them, no less. Cherry is my favorite flavor. I can't wait to taste you on my tongue."

Gggggrrrr! Sweet baby Jesus! You can pop it, eat it, whatever you fucking want.

Cam was still standing at the edge of the bed, by now completely naked. Though it was winter, his skin had a natural, luxuriant bronze glow that made him surpass Adonis in godlike stature. I looked down at his member. The flesh around it was bare and smooth and made his dick look like velvet steel.

I gasped as he essentially ripped off my bra, causing some of the hooks and eyes to tear away. But then as I stared at Cam's blue-veined hammer, I wondered if I could take it all in. It was so big, it almost looked like a separate entity from him. He saw me staring at it all wide-eyed and said, "You like that, don't you? It's all for you—all twelve inches. And I'm going to plunge it deep, deep, deep into you. Get ready."

Oh, shit now. Cameron Sterling has some kink in him.

"Lilly," Cam said deeply, almost growling. He was stroking his twelve inches slowly and deliberately, almost like a warning.

Holy fucking hell! Yes...please, serve me up some Cameron cock any day, anytime, anywhere.

I nodded with giddy affirmation, still totally flabbergasted by the gigantic cock coming my way. His concrete-hard missile pointed almost directly toward the ceiling. His was a heat-seeking missile, and I was its target. He came at me and left no doubt as to what he desired. I was initially overwhelmed by Cam's passionate response and tried to moderate him. But it was not really him I was worried about. I was so aroused that I knew I was going to pop off early, and I did not want to do that. I wanted to pace myself.

"Lover, it's okay. We have plenty of time. There is no need to hurry," I said. But Cam was not hearing me. He wanted to get right down to it. He started right above my navel with raw kisses as he left wet traces behind. He lingered for a bit and then stuck his tongue inside the navel itself. This sent a shockwave to the tip of my clit as his tongue probed the nerve. My abs tightened up with my libido rising to an explosive level. Then his soaking mouth went lower, stopping short of my throbbing clit. He looked up at me, teasing with a mischievous grin.

"You enjoy torturing me, don't you?" I said, resisting the urge to cum right then and there. "Why don't you just do it?"

"You don't tell me when to take what I want. I get it when I'm ready."

I was at Cam's mercy. All I could do was enjoy the seduction as his tongue traced my body all the way back up to my face. He grabbed the curvature of my behind with his fingertips indenting the crease. We were now face to face. Our open mouths met with tongues exploring each other. Cam was so worked up that he started biting like he was eating me. I did not mind. I wanted him to consume me in every way possible. Yeah, at that moment Cameron Sterling was bliss incarnate.

The bulbous, mushroom tip of Cam's throbber rubbed against my clean-shaven box. He kept poking me with his dick, knowing full well that he was only agitating my horniness. My pussy got so very juicy, and I just could not take anymore.

"Please, please, Cam. I…I…want you so bad," I begged.

With strength and vigor, Cam pushed me down on my back. I must admit I looked pretty fucking good the way my hair landed like a halo around my head. I positioned myself into a sexy pose—one leg stretched out, while the other was slightly bent. This way I could open and close them like saloon doors, giving Cam peeks at my nasty bits. I could tell that it was working by the way his luscious mouth was slightly agape with craving.

"Lilly, you by far are the most magnificent creature I have ever seen. I cannot wait to get at you. Spread your legs and let me in."

I did as I was told. The creamy petals of my lips were red and swollen. My clitoris was drenched in my pussy nectar and pulsated so hard it hurt.

"Your pussy looks so beautiful. It looks good enough to eat."

Cam put his mouth right into my cat and rubbed his face all in it. His skin became slick with my sweet ambrosia. His long, eager tongue ran along the length of my slit, from clit to hole, as he took in all the sustenance he needed. He made sure to trace every fold and suck on my delectable clit at well-timed intervals. Pussy juice dripped out of me, but Cam savored it as he licked it all up. The more excited I got, the more I grinded my hips and pulled his face deeper into me. My satisfied moans and the side-to-side tossing of my head let Cam know that he was pleasing me—immensely.

"I want you to cum on my tongue. Then you're going to cum on my cock with that sweet pussy of yours, squeezing me real good," Cam ordered. And I did cum—hard, all over his tongue. Hell, I did not know I was a squirter.

"That pussy tastes so good, I wouldn't mind making a job out of it," Cam said as he licked some of my juice from the corner of his mouth. "Are you ready for some more?" he asked.

"Wait. Just give me a few."

Cam did not listen and primed me instead. He touched my inner thigh lightly because of my ongoing sensitivity. As a result, I felt myself warming up quite nicely and purred a bit. I guess I should not have been surprised. After all, I had been with Sig for so long with no satisfaction that I was now insatiable. How many years had I wasted being doggy fucked by that asshole? Too many. Now it was my turn to get rocked.

Cam's touch turned into kisses and licks. I tingled. "You like that, don't you?" he said as he began kissing my stomach.

Writhing, I responded, "Yes, yes. I want more."

With my senses heightened, my hardened nipples popped out again. I watched Cam. He did not stay in any one spot for too long, but he made sure to avoid the obvious "sexy" parts. This grew my anticipation for a second helping. I had no idea

I had so many erogenous zones. My lubrication started to flow once more.

Cam glanced down. "Your pussy is so swollen. I'm going to take it right now." He took full control and mounted me. Being so close to his face, I could smell my own pussy scent emanating from his mouth. It was savory yet sweet like a peach at the same time. Cam was careful with me at first. He delivered that cock to me one merciful inch at a time, giving my body a chance to accept his massive girth and length. The fullness was almost too much to bear. Every stroke left a devious ache in its wake.

Then Cam started delivering more powerful thrusts. He tore deep inside me and filled me up with that big, thick dick. I did not mind. It hurt so good. Though I was sopping wet, Cam's dick left no room inside of me. It was definitely a tight fight for him. I grabbed his cheeks and spurred him to go even deeper to that sweet spot I did not even know existed.

"Fuck me. Fuck me hard," I moaned. I lost all inhibitions as I bumped my hips against his. Cam's strokes were long and agile. He would pull almost all the way out to the tip of his dick and then go roughly back in, all the way down to his balls. I could feel his tip at the bottom of my lungs, I swear I could. Cam drove in deeper and faster. He grabbed the headboard with one hand for traction.

"Oh, that pussy is so good," he panted.

I started to mildly hyperventilate as passion overtook me. I tightened my legs around Cam's back even more as the intensity of my pleasure almost peaked.

"Not yet. You'll cum when I tell you to cum," Cam said as he noted that I was about to blow. He deepened his strokes and slowed it down. He then painfully bit my nipples while he smirked. This sent a zing straight to my clit. Lord, this man knew what he was doing. I screamed and hoped no one outside would think I was being murdered in the apartment. Sweat burst out of my every pore as my body quaked.

Cam resumed the pace of his previous strokes, pounding into me.

"Harder," I said, an obvious glutton for punishment.

"Lilly," Cam said. He had a hint of concern in his voice regarding the amount of force I desired.

"Cam, please, harder."

"Can't disappoint a lady."

Nearly slamming me through the headboard, Cam pounded his hips into mine. The pain was replaced by total pleasure as I received exactly what I needed. He held my ass with both hands and jackhammered me. He took me to heaven. No, really…I actually saw bright white sparks all around me—fucking stars. And then I came; it could not be stopped. As my scorching pussy pulsed around Cam's dick, he also came. In fact, he came so hard that I could feel his cum as it detonated inside of me with a powerful force.

"Cam! Cam!" I screamed as the walls of my pussy clenched around his cock. My limbs jerked and weakened. Unstable breathing put me on the verge of a panic attack.

Christ on a cross. Can someone have a panic attack from being fucked into oblivion? Shit, I'm having one right now. Oh, God. I think I'm about to pass outtttt…

Then nothing but black.

I woke up to Cam wiping my face with a cool cloth.

"You okay?" he asked, looking at me with concern.

"Yeah, just a little nap."

"No. It was like you fainted."

I remembered what happened. "It was because you felt so damn good. Really."

"And that was me taking it easy on you," Cam said with a lopsided grin.

The fresh memory of our mirrored orgasm made me yearn to be filled once again. As for Cam, he took utter delight in the fact that he made me cum so fucking good and plenty.

We faced each other as we embraced in silence. He just stared at me and was smiling in what could only be described as a hazy dream state. As his warm breath heated my skin, I moved my fingertips along the small of his back. Nothing else existed in the world at that moment except us. I was not only satiated but was finally at peace.

I felt unfamiliar warmth fill me. It brought to mind that saying "time heals all wounds." All of my life, time had been working against me for unknown reasons. My wounds were still raw, gaping, and tender. Until tonight I thought I had hidden them pretty well. Even though Cam did not know the specifics, he somehow picked up on it. Anyway my heart and head had not been separate entities for a long time. They were joined. And they worked together to bully me. Both told me the same thing—that I could never be accepted because of my flaws and past. Whenever I had tried to move on, all I got was tears. I had cried so much that the tears might as well have been thin strands of grass on a dewy morning. Whereas others could feel the wetness of the grass, if I rolled a blade between my fingers, I never felt any wetness on my fingertips. I was numb most of the time. Other times I felt too much. That is what all the pills were for. I was tired of feeling like shit.

However, that night I was there with Cam. It felt cozy, comfortable, and safe. He had given me a gift. Not just his body but a sense of connection to another human being. It had been such a long time since I had that feeling that up until that moment, I could not recollect what it was like. And then it happened. I got scared.

Cam said he wanted to make love to me. What did that mean exactly? Did he mean that he loved me? Yes, I was grateful for this sense of connection with him. However, I was certainly in no position to entertain the thought of love. Besides, over the course of human history, how many men have said the word "love" right before the sex act? A lot. Was I overreacting? Overanalyzing? How could I be sure?

"What's wrong?" Cam asked. Damn, my ambivalence was all over my face.

"Nothing," I responded as I mentally calculated the outcome of a myriad of future probabilities. Shit, I had no idea where all this was headed.

I was not naïve, though. Cam and I had crossed the line big time. Now, no matter what course we took, there was going to be some kind of danger up ahead. Someway, somehow, somebody was going to get hurt.

But I decided that for once I was not going to go berserk over words, overthinking everything. I had so few good times in my life, and here I was actually experiencing one. I was going to just indulge in the rest of this resplendent moment and enjoy being with this awesome man. However, I was still terrified.

I worried that I had come off like a bitch. It had been a couple of hours since Cam said he wanted to make love to me, and I was still ruminating over it. Now he slept next to me in what appeared to be the most peaceful slumber. But before he had drifted off, once again he asked me if I was happy. I skirted the question, of course. However, Cam almost did not let me get away with it. He took my face into his hands, kissed me, and asked again. I almost succumbed and spilled my soul, but thankfully he told me that I did not have to answer right then.

My aloof reaction must have seemed strange to Cam. But the fact remained that I was someone else's woman. I tried to relay my feelings of guilt by telling myself that it was not my intention to sleep with Cam; I just wanted to say hello and have a friendly afternoon chat. That was bullshit, and I knew it. I must have fantasized about screwing him at least thirty times that day. I planned the whole thing.

Cam had to make it all the more difficult by giving me the best sex of my life. To top it all off, I really did have some kind of feelings for him. There was no way I could deny it. However, my greatest fear bubbled up. This fear haunted me my whole life. That fear was that Cam was enamored with the illusion of who I pretended to be. So many times before, so-called love arrived but jettisoned away as my fatal flaws came to the surface. If Cam got to know the real me, I was sure he would abandon me like everyone else I cared about did. I could not take another heartbreak.

The other problem was Sig. I did not have any real love for him. However, emotions never provided security or career success. Besides, being involved with Cam was risky. I really did not know him; we had only seen each other a few times over the course of a couple weeks. What was to say that this fling would last? Right now, at that moment, Cam looked like a prime prospect, but I could not be sure. At least I knew what I was getting with Sig. There was no guesswork. I already knew who he was, and he had provided me with many advantages. When it came down to Sig or Cam, it was not so much superficial considerations. It was about survival.

Cam rustled about and sighed contently. I knew that if I never went home to Sig, Cam would be fine with it. I cannot say that idea was not tempting. I wrestled with the urge to stay there in his bed and never go back to Sig's mansion. But my dark shadow reminded me that I was a for-shit human being and that I had better get out of there before Cam caught on. I hopped out of bed and tried to sneak out. However, Cam woke up.

"Hey, sweetie, what are you doing?" he asked in that fucking sexy-as-hell, groggy voice.

"I've got to get home. Before Sig does," I said, putting my shirt on inside out. I could see the disappointment on Cam's face.

"Really? You're actually going back there? After what just happened?"

"Cam, I can't stay. You know that. You've known the reality of this situation since the beginning." Cam hopped out of bed. I lost my breath at the sight of his chiseled, naked body. I wanted more.

"I've got to go right now. Or else," I rambled, hopping to put on one of my shoes.

"Or else what?"

I was tongued-tied as Cam walked toward me. I backed up, right into a wall, trying to avoid his seduction. I swear I actually felt myself melt into it. Cam grabbed me hard and kissed me. I might as well have been underwater drowning because that is what it felt like. My chest was heavy with newly aroused desire. I could not breathe. I became limp and so lightheaded I almost passed out. I got away from him by scooting along the wall to the front door. I fiddled with the doorknob behind me, so butterfingered that I could not twist it open.

"Oh, God, Cameron, I gotta go right now," I said. I was practically pleading for him to stop enticing me. I finally managed to open the door and ran out of that loft. Cam wrapped a sheet around his waist and pursued me.

I made it down the stairs so fast it was like I Star Trekked it from the upper to lower level. However, athletic Cam had no trouble catching up to me as I made it to my car. It did not concern him that he was outside butt naked, draped in only a thin sheet. I slung open the car door, but Cam shut it before I could get in.

"You don't have to leave. You can stay here," he said, seemingly unaffected by the blistering cold wind.

I just looked at him. The expression on my face revealed that he was trying to force me to make a difficult choice. Cam relented and opened the door for me. I got in and started the engine. He stood outside looking at me, still beckoning me to stay. I let the window down.

"I'm sorry," I said with true remorse. Cam leaned in and kissed me on my forehead.

"Lilly, when you need me, I'll be here. You count on that."

"I know. That's part of the problem."

Cam looked perplexed. "Problem? What problem?"

"Look at you, Cam. Standing out here like the hero. Can't you understand that if you were a jerk, it would be so much easier to leave?"

"So if I spit on your windshield, you would stay?" he joked.

"No, but I do have to go. Good-bye, Cam."

It took everything I had to drive away. I watched him grow smaller in my rearview mirror and lost sight when I turned a corner. All the way home I fought with myself. The greater part of me wanted to turn around and go back to Cam. But the rational part kept me headed home. Besides, it was better this way. Cam still had an idealized version of me. I did not want to mess that up.

The drive went by too fast. I got home with a couple of waking hours left. Hopefully Sig would not be there. I did not have the fortitude to deal with him. But as bad luck would have it, I saw him standing on the front steps, waiting for me. I took my time driving up, giving myself time to spritz on some perfume to cover Cam's scent, which was still clinging to my body.

I entered the circular driveway directly in front of the house and parked. Sig was no gentleman and had no intentions of opening my car door for me. All he did was glare with warranted suspicion. I got out of the car and made sure to keep my eyes from landing on his by pretending to look for something in my purse.

"Hello, Sig. What're you doing standing out here in the cold?" I said, still rummaging through my Hermes bag.

"Where have you been? You did not tell me that you would be out, and I have been calling for the past few hours," he snarled.

I reached for the doorknob, trying to get as far away from

him as I could. "Really? I must have had the phone on vibrate. I had an early lunch with Tamara. Then I just hung out in the city for a bit. It's so beautiful in the winter time, you know."

Sig held the door closed so I could not go into the house. He sniffed around me like a hound dog. Suddenly he delivered an open-hand slap to my cheek, knocking me to the cold ground. It was so hard that it rang my ears and caused momentarily blindness.

"You fucking…nasty…filthy liar! Did you actually think I could not smell another man on you? You reek of him. Who is he?"

"There's no one. No one else. I swear. I'm all yours," I said, crying and lying my ass off.

"You know why I keep you around? It is not because I love you. I do not even like you. I keep you around because you are my property; you belong to me to do with as I please. And as my property, I own you forever. If you ever think about leaving me or seeing your lover again, just know that I will find out. But do not worry; I will not kill *you* for it. I will kill *him* in your place. Make no mistake, I will have him tortured and killed right in front of you. As for your pretty face, acid can rearrange it quite nicely. Now get inside."

I got up slowly, making sure not to appear aggressive or spook Sig in any way. He followed close behind me as I made my way to the bedroom. I tried to show no signs of fear or retaliation, for he was an animal and would react to it appropriately. I knew that I could not be as reckless as I was that afternoon because Cam's life could be at stake. And knowing Sig like I did, I knew that his threat was real. I had no doubt of his ability to follow through.

Sig kept watch over me like a prison guard. The only way to escape him was to go to the bathroom. I shut the door and locked it. The mirror was taunting me to look into it. I did. Staring back at me was a battered and bruised reflection, not only my skin but my spirit.

There was some blood in my mouth as a result of biting my cheek when Sig hit me. I spit it out and rinsed the sink. I envied the red spiral of blood draining away into oblivion. I wished I could escape with it. Hell, I even longed to return to that shithole I came from—back to my daddy—which I swore I would never do.

Oh, who was I kidding? I deserved that slap. No matter what wool I pulled over Cam's eyes, I was still a nobody. Worse than a nobody. I was nothing.

I ran water for a bath and downed two Prozac. As I sank into the steamy water, I felt Cam rinsing off me. I fishtailed my hand through the water as Cam's essence floated in the clear liquid. That put a smile on my face, but it dissolved just as fast as it came. The gears in my heart were in overdrive, and I had no idea how to get them back to neutral. I became nauseous at the thought of never seeing him again.

But I had to let Cam go. Or else he might die.

Chapter Thirteen

I was under the impression that Mr. Wotherspoon and I were going to have a general meeting. But as I entered his office, I was surrounded by undercover detectives and Chief Pepperdine, the chief of police. As always, Xander crept in the corner, watching me like he wanted to pull my fingernails out.

"Yes, Mr. Wotherspoon? You wanted to see me," I said as the others watched me curiously. By his relaxed mannerisms, I could see that Mr. Wotherspoon was way too familiar with these law enforcement officials. Moreover, I felt like I was being set up for something. A disconcerting knot clenched in my belly as Wotherspoon uncharacteristically put his arm around my shoulder.

"This is Cameron Sterling, the newest member of our elite little club. Get to know this one because he is going places," Mr. Wotherspoon said to the others, and then he addressed me. "Cam, these men are an invisible part of the Wotherspoon team. They help us out with special favors and protection. Think of them as our clandestine friends pulling all the right strings behind the scenes for us."

"Now that you have been initiated, I take it that we will have a symbiotic relationship where all benefit from the union. A perfect brotherhood," Chief Pepperdine said as he put his arm around my other shoulder. I felt my asshole tighten up in anticipation of some secretive gay rite like the ones I had read about on the Internet.

"No, no. Cam has not been fully initiated yet, but he is well on his way. He is working on the Sig Krok case," Mr. Wotherspoon explained as he walked away from me. The police chief and detectives nodded like they had some insider information I was not hip to.

Mr. Wotherspoon picked up a stack of files that had Sig's name written on all the tabs. What made this notable was that the firm had a strict color-coding system, and these files were white. Never in all my years at Wotherspoon and Associates had I ever seen white files.

"Cam, today you are going to meet with Mr. Krok. He has mentioned some personal problems at home. Since he has paid us handsomely, we will go over and above to help him out in whatever way we can. We cannot afford to have one of our bricks fall out of the wall. Our success is intimately connected with his—and also with his failure."

"What exactly is Sig's problem?" I asked as if I did not know.

"He believes his wife is cheating on him," Chief Pepperdine said.

The last person I wanted to see was Sig, but I had not heard from Lilly since we made love. She had not responded to any of my texts or voicemails. I wondered if she had gotten cold feet. Maybe I could surreptitiously find out from Sig how she was doing.

"All right. When and where?" I asked.

Mr. Wotherspoon gave me the specifics while he opened a hidden safe behind a picture. He must have been distracted because he tapped in his code right in front of me. I got all the digits.

Really, Mr. Wotherspoon? Your birthday. How lame.

There was only one number that I missed—the last one.

―――

Zagat could not rate The Fordham Steakhouse high enough. Devoid of the annoying hipster crowd, The Fordham catered to an upper-crust clientele who relished in the subdued yet elegant environment. Low lighting, burgundy accents, and dark wood paneling created an atmosphere of understated sophistication. The polished wait staff dressed in black pants and vests accented with stark white shirts. The white linen napkins draped over their arms added a special touch. Just as smug as the gilt-edged diners, they proudly served the best whites and reds as well as lobster and perfectly aged beef.

I was hoping to arrive before Sig, but the hostess informed me that he was already there. She led me past small groups of ambitious businessmen, power brokers, and old-money spinsters to a large booth at the back of the restaurant where Sig had taken up residence.

"Nice to see you again, Mr. Krok," I said as I extended my hand. Sig did not return the favor.

Sig had always looked at me with an icy stare, but today it was more frigid than usual. "The pleasure is all mine, Mr. Sterling. I hope you don't mind. I took the liberty of ordering for the both of us."

I could see that he was trying to take the alpha dog role. Whatever. I decided that I would go along with his nonsense, not revealing any of my playbook. "That's fine. I'm sure you have exquisite taste in food like everything else," I said.

"Like Lilly," Sig responded.

A chill went up my spine. I looked at him a little more closely. Behind his eyes I saw that he still suspected something was going on between Lilly and me. I wondered if that was why I had not heard from her. Did Sig get to her?

"Like Lilly," I said. "Also like your empire, which we are trying to protect."

Sig's mouth twitched. He knew I was diverting attention away from Lilly, trying to control the direction of the conversation.

I said, "I have been over some of your records, and I have found some things that need explanation. There are certain purchases made for the individual named Z that have been listed as business expenditures." I pulled out some of the records and slid them over to Sig. "But they sure don't look like business to me. Mr. Krok, these are personal."

I waited for him to flinch. However, he just sat there with no apparent look of concern. Sig knew he was basically untouchable, and my involvement in the case was a mere formality. What Sig wanted, though, was to manipulate me into spilling the beans about Lilly and me.

He said, "You know that I am a man of means, don't you? And whether we call those purchases business or personal does not matter. Take Lilly, for instance. I spend money on her. It is personal because she is my girlfriend. However, it is also business because as much as I hate to admit it, she has enhanced Klå. Either way I have bought and paid for her. She is mine."

My fists balled up under the table. I was a hair's breath away from jumping across it and beating the smirk off Sig's face. "No disrespect, but I'm sure Lilly has a different perspective on your association."

Sig gave me the crooked smile of a maniac. "Lilly has no problem with our arrangement. Gold-digging social climbers never do. Haven't you thought about why she is with me? I'm significantly older than her and admittedly not much to look at. But what I lack in youth and physical appeal, I make up for with success and money. Because of me, Lilly keeps the best company and can buy whatever her heart desires. Once women like her get used to the type of lifestyle I have provided, they never go backward."

I knew Sig was right. I had seen too many wives of wealthy clients put up with all sorts of bullshit in exchange for mansions, jewels, and luxury vacations. Love could indeed be bought. What I learned about Lilly through the media was that she had a habit of dating increasingly more powerful men. Even though I was an attorney, financially and socially I would be a step down from Sig Krok.

"There is also that thing with Lilly's father," Sig said as he took a sip of tea. "He was a pedophile."

I was aghast, mortified at what I was hearing. But my mind would not let it register. I obviously did not hear Sig correctly. "Come again?"

"Oh, do not act as if you were born yesterday. Things like that happen all the time. No, Lilly's father never had sex with her. He only beat her every day of her childhood. Put her in the hospital several times. Her mother covered it up. Lilly ended up with a nasty little drug habit during her adolescent and teen years because of it. She kicked it, but not without a stint in the mental ward. After she was declared fit, she started modeling. But she is still a psych case if you ask me. If anyone knew the real Lilly, they would run for the hills."

Goddamn. I had such a visceral reaction that I felt like I was being dismembered right at that table. Lilly had so many secrets. What else was she hiding from me? Fuck, I had my own demons to fight, let alone trying to help someone else battle theirs.

Our waitress delivered our food: porterhouse steaks delicately seasoned with sea salt and peppercorns, tender steamed asparagus, and fluffy buttermilk mashed potatoes. The decadent meal sent a desirous shudder through me, but I was not about to eat the food of my enemy. My reluctance to eat did not make any difference to Sig, however. He sliced into his extremely blue-rare steak and lapped the piece around in the blood puddle.

Sig said, "Do you know what people need? It is not air, food, water, not even God. It is money. People will die and kill for it. The wealthy like me would not stoop to die for money. But we most certainly will kill for it."

I really was not in the mood for Sig's games. I just wanted to know how Lilly was. "What is your point, Sig?" I asked, trying to move the menacing conversation along.

He held up his fork and admired the bloody meat. "The point of all that money is to control other people. That is what people like me do. We do not know how to operate in any other way. You see, money and the promise of fame is how I maintain my hold on Lilly. But it has come to my attention that she has taken on a lover. Whoever he is, he has pissed on my tree.

Fortunately, I have Wotherspoon and Associates. They have assured me that my happiness is their priority. As you know, your firm has a steady connection to law enforcement. And that Xander...he is a prince. I have heard many tales about his exploits—like something about a missing associate named Gene Byrd. So when I find out who the other man is, he will be destroyed in every way possible. I will personally see to it. As a side note, I will do terrible, terrible things to Lilly, too, for having betrayed my trust. I have the means to get away with just about anything."

Then Sig shoved the chunk of steak in his mouth. He chewed it like a cat that just caught a mouse as he eyeballed me. I could not be sure if he was threatening me or just being himself. But I did know that staying away from Lilly might be the most loving act I could perform for her.

———

My cheek was still red and slightly swollen from Sig's slap, and I was nursing it with a cold compress.

Under normal conditions I would have been thankful to have the house all to myself. But Sig was in town having lunch with Cam. I was anxious about their meeting. Cam was in love with me, and I worried that he would confront Sig with the true nature of our relationship. Plus I really wanted to be at that lunch too, sans Sig. I desperately missed Cam. I wanted to hold him, kiss him, and tell him that I was sorry for bringing him into my chaotic life.

I had to distract myself or else I would have gone totally insane. I decided that I needed some aromatherapy and headed for one of many linen closets for some candles. But something struck me as I passed Sig's office. I peered inside and could see the memory of Sig ghost sitting at his computer, his face consumed with sexual desire. So many times I had stumbled upon him typing with fury as he engaged in some illicit Internet chat with some other lover.

For a second I felt hurt by the remembrance of his indiscretion, but that was quickly replaced by indignation. How dare that motherfucker? I was faithful to him the entire time we had been together, barring the time I had recently spent with Cam. Shit, I suddenly felt justified for screwing Cam because of all the crap Sig had put me through. He was lucky that fucking Cam was the worst thing I had done. Sig deserved so much more.

It was about time I grew some balls and found out who Sig was chatting with. I raised the lid on his computer and immediately went into snoop mode. But I could not access any information. I did not know his password, which he changed nearly every day. It didn't matter anyway because I heard Sig's limo driving across the rocks in front of the house. I peeked outside and saw the chauffeur letting him out.

I positioned Sig's computer back into the exact spot I found it and wiped off my fingerprints. Like a frog hyped up on sugar, I leaped into the kitchen in one fell swoop. I leaned against the counter as if I had been standing there the whole time. I tensed up as I watched the door. I would know if Sig knew about Cam and me by whether he came in with his usual snarl or a gun instead.

The doorknob creaked as it was turned as slowly as a sloth crawling through syrup. I gripped the countertop a little tighter with dreaded anticipation. I swear Sig was taking his time just to be dramatic. *Such a fucking queen.* He finally entered. The snarky expression and sucking of his yellow-ass, cakey teeth let me know just how enthused he was to see me. But aside from his pout and urgent need for dental care, I could not make out anything else going on in that mind of his. I took it upon myself to break the silence.

"So how was your day? Was your meeting with Cam productive?" *Shit.* My voice cracked while trying to fake Sig out. I knew I had pushed my luck and that Sig sniffed out my pitiful ruse.

"What do you care about my meeting with Mr. Sterling? You have no reason to concern yourself with my business. *Do you?*"

"No, I was just wondering how my boyfriend's day went."

"I bet you were," Sig said. There was an undertone in his voice that inferred that Cam was really the one who was my boyfriend. He looked at me, waiting for my face to tell the truth about the nature of my relationship with Cam. I was tired of playing games with this old man. It took a massive amount of self-control not to tell him that Cam had given me the best fucking day—and when I say fucking, I literally mean fucking—of my whole life. *In your face, Sig. To hell with you. Now what?* But instead of going off like I was on Steve Wilkos's stage, I played it cool and gave Sig the sweetest smile I could muster.

With the situation diffused, Sig backed off. "I have to make an emergency trip to Thailand tomorrow. One of the factories is having some issues. You can't go."

Oh, motherfucker. As if I wanted to.

"That's totally okay. I understand," I said as I tried to curb a gigantic "yippee" that was a hair's breadth away from slipping off my tongue. Sig just did not know that I was pretty much popping bottles anytime he went out of town. That is when I was free from his spindly-fingered grip. Hell, the only time the stank bitch ever took me on trips was for show, to promote his perfect boyfriend image.

However, out of nowhere, one naughty chortle escaped my mouth. Sig menaced toward me and sneered, "Yes, I am sure my absence will cause you no distress. It gives you the chance to do whatever—or whoever—you would like." Sig put four fingers behind my neck and kept his thumb on my larynx. "I do not trust you, Lilly. Not one bit. I know you have another lover. But you think you are so smart…that you've covered your tracks."

I shook my neck out of Sig's cold embrace and backed into the counter. Looking at his putrid face made me want to punch him square in the nose. He looked so much like my father. The more I saw the resemblance, the more paralyzed I became. With those glacial eyes and lifeless, bleached skin, Sig could easily pass for my father's brother.

"I already told you. There is no one else," I stuttered.

"Like I said, when I find out who he is, I will rain fire down upon both of you. So if you care anything about your piece of dick, you better leave him alone."

Sig thought I was weak. And he was right about that. But he also thought I was profoundly dumb. As if I had no clue as to why he was really going to Thailand. I knew the trip was a guise. It was an excuse to spend time with *his* lover without the prying eyes of the American paparazzi or me finding out.

I had finally reached a tipping point concerning his double standard. Sig could have a jump-off while I am supposed to only get ass fucked by him? That was some bullshit.

My pussy had enjoyed being serviced by Cam and wanted some more. And that same pussy gave me a teensy bit of backbone and forced me to speak up for her. "Even if I was screwing someone else, who are you to have any say so?" my channeled pussy said. "You...on your computer all the time. With your secrets. Why are you so worried about what I'm doing? Who the shit are you fucking?"

Okay, pussy, calm the hell down. You're going to get us both killed in here.

Pussy said back to me, *Oh, no. This fool needs to know.*

Sig stepped backward, almost stumbling, not believing the words spewing from my acrid tongue. I stood there with my eyes wide as fuck too; I was in disbelief myself.

"What did you just say to me?" Sig asked like an executioner about to drop the blade of a guillotine.

My face had just healed up, and I did not want to get hit again. "Nothing."

"What?" Sig said as he grabbed my face.

"Nothing, Sig, nothing."

I longed to fight back. But my insecurities made my fists limp and weakened my voice. I understood that he was not my true enemy, just one of many manifestations of two foes. The foes I could not defeat were the haunting memories of my past and the knowledge that I was nothing special. In fact, I was subpar. I had to be. Otherwise no one would have even thought to hurt me like they did when I was a child. If I were special or worthy, other people would have seen it, especially my father.

The one person who should have loved and protected me the most. But I reasoned that I had to be truly fucked up if not even my own father could love me. That is why my feet stayed planted as Sig tore into my soul.

Satisfied with his win, Sig released me. Then Lin came in to mop the kitchen. She abruptly stopped as she caught the tail end of my chastisement. I saw that look of pity on her face. It was so ironic that I was hailed as the lucky one to outsiders—so rich, so beautiful. But the truth was that this housekeeper was so much greater than me.

"Go upstairs and pack my clothes," Sig ordered Lin. She nodded in compliance and started out of the kitchen but turned back and looked at my shamed face. Her eyes showed so much fear for me. But more than that I saw my reflection in the darkness of Lin's eyes, and I did not like what I saw. I was jarred, shaken up. A gigantic fissure cracked inside me. A lightning-strike epiphany suddenly bolted through my skull. I had wasted too much time feeling sorry for myself. All the ruminating about the past, my father, and stupid self-worth issues had taken a toll on me. I was an empty vessel. Thank goodness for Cam. That man resuscitated me. Now it was my turn.

I was standing at that proverbial fork in the road with no map or GPS. I could not turn back and keep repeating the same sob story. Shit, that tome was starting to bore even me. To go forward would require the courage to admit that if I remained screwed up, it was my own doing. I had to make a change. Even if I never saw Cam again, I still would have been grateful because the short time we were together opened my eyes to other realities. Mind you, I still wanted that spokesmodel spot. Fuck, I earned that with blood and tears. But I also wanted so much more. A life with no more fear, anxiety, or those god-damn pills. I knew where all of this was heading. Eventually I would have to take a stand.

Suddenly I was jolted out of contemplation by Sig's demanding voice.

"What are you looking at? Why are you still standing there? Get my clothes ready…now," Sig said to Lin.

Lin lingered at the door for a moment as if beckoning me to leave with her. She wanted so badly to rescue me. I just low-ered my head; I could not even look her in the eye. Lin showed sympathy by choosing not to prolong my embarrassment. She disappeared into the house, while Sig poured himself a glass of wine.

"I've got so many people on my payroll, people who can make sure you disappear. You must know by now that nobody can help you," Sig said as he made his way to the door. He put his hand on the doorframe and chuckled as if he heard the funniest joke ever. "And no one can help him either. Whoever he is."

Sig took a swig of his wine and sauntered out. Left alone in the kitchen, I was quickly filled with a sense of exhilaration. Maybe I could actually have another life? A smile crossed my face as I lightly danced around the kitchen, contemplating the infinity possibilities. However, in midtwirl, a wrenching pain seared through my belly. I recognized that pain immediately. It was the first sign of a genuine panic attack, not like that fainting spell I had at Cam's. I tried to breathe my way out of it, but that did nothing except make me gasp for air even harder. The room started to wobble, and I veered into a wall for support.

Would I ever be able to overcome this anxiety? Not today. Anybody for a Xanax cocktail?

Chapter Fourteen

The backs of my closed eyelids looked red from the glare of the morning sun. I opened my eyes, nearly blinded by the bright light, and then rolled over toward the empty side of the bed. I wished that Lilly were there. The separation had taken its toll on me. I was cranky, could not focus at work, and did not have the fortitude to eat a decent meal in some days.

Despite the disparaging things Sig told me about Lilly, I still could not quench my desire to see her again. Maybe she had overcome her demons. I mean Sig was not exactly the truthful type. And I knew he had an inkling that I bedded Lilly. That fucker probably would tell all sorts of lies to keep me from her.

Still half asleep, I was on autopilot. Instinct made me pick up my cell phone and dial Lilly's number. If I had been fully awake, I am not so sure I would have done that. I was not only taking a chance with my career but risking my life. I did not care. I wanted to talk to her, and nothing was going to stop me. The phone rang for a long time, and I was about to hang up. Then an angelic voice came over the airwaves.

"Hello. Cam?" Lilly said.

"Lilly?"

"Of course. Were you trying to reach someone else? I can hang up." She had the cutest laugh to accompany her lame attempt at humor.

"No, no, no. You are exactly the person I want to talk to. Can you talk?"

"Yeah. Sig is out of town."

I did a "yes" arm pump. "Great. When can I come over?"

Lilly let go of an uncomfortable snort. "Cam, I think Sig knows about us. As much as I want to see you, I can't. I don't want you to get hurt."

"I see Sig threatened you too. Look, I promise to never see or talk to you again if you can honestly tell me that you don't want me."

The silence from the other end let me know that Lilly was trying to come up with some excuse or, better yet, lie. But she could not say that she did not want me.

"Cam, why are you doing this to me?" Lilly asked.

"Doing what to you?"

"Making me choose between you and Sig."

"I'm not asking for a commitment. Just some of your time. Look, I know you're lonely and scared about the future. You don't have to think about that. Let's just have a good time. Just dinner. No pressure. How about it?"

Lilly played it coy, hesitating for a few moments. She was torturing me by making me wait for her to answer. She said, "There's no harm in dinner, right? Anyway what Sig doesn't know won't hurt him."

―――

I waited for Cam amid a shower of snow shimmering against the daylight. A sliver of a breath mint bounced around my mouth. I wondered if I was being presumptuous, assuming I was going to get a kiss. This was *just* supposed to be dinner—an early one apparently as it was just after 2:00 p.m. Just in case something else went down, I made sure to put on the most amazing cocktail dress I had. Underneath my sheepskin coat was a strapless Vera Wang, definitely more of a summer dress. But I thought, *Fuck it. It's crazy sexy.* Amazingly, the frostbite-inducing temperature had no effect on me at all. That is because lurid thoughts about Cam kept me warm.

A flutter of butterflies tickled my insides as my anticipation grew exponentially with each passing minute. I rocked on my feet as I craned my neck looking down the long driveway. I was surprised that I had absolutely no guilt about what I was doing. However, I was a bit frustrated that I had let myself go for so long without this type of satisfaction while living with Sig. I had missed out on so much—fun, excitement, and ultimate pleasure. Why had I limited myself? Why had I not demanded more? Fuck me for letting Sig take the best of me and use it up like a dirty napkin.

The rumble of Cam's motorcycle made its presence known before any visual contact was made. I took a deep breath to calm myself down and to not appear too anxious. But it was not working. The truth was that I was a complete nervous wreck. I started to feel myself trembling. My pussy started to moisten, some kind of Pavlov's dog reaction to Cam.

The motorcycle rounded the bend. When Cam came into view, I saw that he was dressed way more casually than me. He sported an obsidian leather jacket, dark jeans, and Doc Martens. He looked like a black knight riding up on his steel steed. I know I should have been upset that he was what I considered terribly underdressed. But he looked so good; I could not help but cut him some slack.

I approached Cam as he parked in front of the house. "So

what's this? You know they have dress codes at five-star restaurants nowadays," I said with mock irritation.

Cam rose off the bike and lifted his helmet off. The heat had glossed his hair, and he slicked it back with his hands. While he did that, his deep-set eyes swept over my body as he smiled that smirky grin. Swoon.

"You must have mistaken me for someone else. I never said we were going to some hoity-toity place."

"So where are you taking me? Burger King?" I opened my coat to let Cam see my outfit as an indication of the type of restaurant I was expecting to go to.

"Hey, Burger King! I didn't think about that. That's actually a good idea."

Cam thought he was being funny, but I started to actually become irritated with his glib attitude. Shit, I did not get dressed up for nothing. "Really, where are we going?"

Cam looked at me perplexed, and then a sardonic expression crossed his face. He pointed at the mansion and said, "So you've bought into this fantasy? You're basically just some coddled couch poodle?"

Seriously? Cam was goading me and enjoying every second of it. What the fuck was that all about? I, on the other hand, took total offense. I should have told him to get the hell off my property but…damn it. Why did he have to look so good? Shit, who was I trying to fool? I was still going to dinner with this sexy asshole. But first I would have to play it off.

"Well, I do feel sorry for you," I said, trying to put him in an underdog position.

He smirk-laughed. "Really? You feel sorry for me? I got to hear this."

"You wanted to take me out and drove all the way out here just to spend some time together. Obviously you missed me. And here I am, basically rejecting your romantic overture. You must think I am so shallow."

Good mind fuck, Lilly.

But Cam was too smart to fall for my manipulation. He put his helmet back on without any discussion. I stood there with my arms crossed, waiting for him to come to his senses. However, when he threw his leg over the seat, I saw that he was really leaving. Confounded, I rushed over to him.

"Where are you going?" I asked, my voice beseeching. Cam took off his helmet and looked at me, trying to figure out what the fuck my problem was.

"I asked you out because I had a great time the other night and genuinely wanted to see you again. I thought you were cool. But instead I get this game playing. You can save that bullshit for Sig because I have no tolerance for that."

Cam was right. I had let him down. I had spent too much time pretending to be some other woman. "She" was the one who just had that hissy fit—not me. I had forgotten what it was like to be honest with another person. I knew that the real me did not want to mess up my one chance at happiness. It was time to start shedding the façade and let the true me come out. But who was I? Shit, I could not even remember. I just had fragmented memories of who I used to be…the long-gone good part of me. Mercifully, something in my soul relented and allowed some repressed humbleness to break through.

"I'm sorry. I was being rude…my alter ego," I said.

"Your alter ego is a bitch." Cam laughed. He thought my comment was a joke. Sadly, he did not realize how real she was.

"So are you still going to feed me?" I asked.

"Of course. But you do realize that I had something else in mind," Cam said as he subtly yet suggestively grazed his colossal erection. I swear to God I tried so hard not to react, not give him the satisfaction. However, I found my careless tongue sweep from one side to the other. Somehow I managed to force it back in but not without serious effort, and I had to draw in a much-needed breath to calm down.

Damn it. Why does this man have to be so sticky delicious?

A wry smile crossed Cam's face as his pointed finger made reference to my clothing. "You need to change," he said.

Okay, Cam might have looked good, but I did too. I kept my coat open, waiting for at least a compliment. But he gestured toward the front door instead. "Go on in now and change. You want to eat, don't you?"

What? Seriously? Okay, I know that I was being an ass before. But I was totally mortified that Cam did not even notice how fucking fantastic I looked. Old habits die hard, and I felt my fragile alter ego rising up again. She was used to receiving endless compliments. That is how she thrived. Cam was testing her by not fawning. She wanted to tell him to fuck off. But the real me was hungry as hell, and there was nothing prepared in the house. And, God help me, Cam did look so good.

For the first time I told my alter ego to shut the fuck up. She was not going to ruin this. I snatched my coat closed and clomped to the door but not too hard. I was not about to destroy my Jimmy Choos for anyone, including Cam.

"I'll be right back," I said. My alter ego wrestled with me all the way to the front door. She told me I was a punk for letting Cam get the upper hand. She argued me down about how he thought I was an insignificant nobody who did not deserve the best in life, and that was why he was not taking me to a fancy restaurant, that he was going to serve me slop from a trough. But I took my alter ego by the neck and put a sleeper hold on her. I knew it would only render her unconscious for the night. But the night was all I needed.

As I was about to duck into the house, Cam said, "By the way, you look beautiful. You've got me all worked up over here. Hurry. I don't know how long I can take being away from you."

Oh, that did it. I knew that this date was supposed to be just dinner. But if Cam wanted it, he was so getting fucked tonight. I tried to play it like TLC…you know, crazysexycool. But when I tried to walk into the house, I ran into the door instead. I looked back at Cam and gave him the old "I meant to do that" look then clumsily went inside.

"It is so chilly. You can come inside too, you know," I said, trying to erase his memory of me slamming my face in the door.

"No. I don't want to go in Sig's house unless it is absolutely necessary." Cam was kind of chuckling. I could tell he was amused by my face whack. Talk about being embarrassed.

"Suit yourself," I said as I tried to maintain a composed front. "I'll be right back." I shut the door and leaned back on it. I lightly beat the back of my head on the panel. I still could not believe how bumbling I was. *Stupid. Stupid. Stupid.*

But there was no time to mull over my blunder. I had a hunk of a man waiting for me outside. I practically ran right out of my Jimmy Choos and went up the stairs two at a time. I made it to my bedroom and scampered to the back of my closet. As I pulled out some casual clothing, I saw the handle of a suitcase peeking out from underneath some random boxes. I forgot that was even there. It had been secretly packed for years. When I first got it, I told myself an untruth. I said that I only had it just in case I wanted to go on an impromptu vacation. But deep inside I knew it was ready just in case I got up the courage to leave Sig. Was tonight that night?

No, it was not. Cam did not invite me to live with him. It was just dinner. But the magic in the air made me want to grab that suitcase, run out with it, and beg Cam to take me away from all of that madness. I pushed the suitcase further back into the closet, making sure it would not be discovered by Sig.

Maybe some other time, I thought. I sighed at the idea and then got right back to my clothing change. I flipped through every pair of jeans I owned—all Klå, mind you. Except one pair. I had kept my near-decade-old Levi's 501s. They looked like redheaded stepchildren next to the perfectly crafted Klå jeans. They had a rubbed hole on the knee, frazzled hems, and were faded quite a bit. However, they were skin tight, acting as the perfect shapewear for my ass and thighs.

Besides, I loved those jeans even though Sig despised them. He thought they were lowbrow, a sign of inferior breeding. I did not care about all that. I had bought those Levi's when I had a moment of hope that things could actually turn out well for me. Though that fleeting moment disappeared fast, I wore those jeans like my life depended on it, hoping that the promising future they offered would someday come to pass. So far the only thing I got was Sig. But now Cam was waiting for me outside. Maybe he and I would not have forever, but at least I could experience one happy night in those jeans.

I slipped on the Levi's, a turtleneck, and a pair of boots. As I quickly touched up my makeup, the Xanax, Prozac, and

Klonopin loomed in my peripheral vision. I tried to ignore their presence, but they whispered to me, pretending they were friends. They beckoned me to put them in my purse and take them with me. After all, I would need some help being funny and engaging. I had no way of doing that on my own. I tried to ignore the temptation. I wanted to try to be me, the real me. Not that fake, doped-up mirage. But the drugs told me I could not do it. There was no way I could hack being normal for a change.

Quickly, I walked to the bedroom door and placed my hand on the knob. The drugs called to me again. *This is your last chance. Do you want Cam to know what you really are?* I closed my eyes and tried to draw in strength. It did not work. I relented to the drugs and retrieved them from the bathroom. I stuck them in my purse.

Just in case. I won't use them. I swear to God I won't use them.

Was I simply weak or unwilling to give up my prescription crutches? Really, they did not help me one iota; they just kept me circling a loop. I was still a mess. The only way to get out of it was to confront my past. The evil that lurked back there was a monster I still could not face. Until I did, it would own me—mind, body, and soul.

As I walked to the front door, I could see Cam through the window. He was a beacon lighting my way. The closer I got to him, the better I started to feel. When I stepped outside, Cam took my hand and led me to his motorcycle.

I confessed, "I've never been on a bike before."

"That's okay. Just put your hands on my hips, and I'll do the rest. Don't worry. I'll take very good care of you."

"Where are we going, anyway?"

Cam kissed me to squash any interrogation I might have had in mind. But his kiss had another effect all together. It made all my nerves stand at attention. He instantly rekindled all the intoxicating desire from our previous tryst. His hard kiss was interspersed with soft nips and pecks. I grabbed the lapel of his shirt and pulled him in closer to me.

"We can do it right here," I proposed.

"I have something better in mind. But let's have dinner first." If Cam thought that would tamp down my wanton desire, he was grossly mistaken. I relented and decided to go along with Cam's plans for the evening.

Cam securely fastened the spare helmet on my head and helped me mount the bike. He instructed me to put my feet on the foot pegs right before he got on. He then started the bike. It reverberated under me like having sex on a washing machine. Cam revved the engine, and we were off.

The ride was by no means light and leisurely. Cam was aggressive, and we sped down winding back roads and a rollercoaster of hills. The motorcycle leaned almost to the pavement as he made tight turns. Fear sat in my throat, but I was enlivened by the way my life teetered on the two-wheeled apparatus. I had traveled through this same scenery hundreds of times, but it never looked as appealing as it did that afternoon—though it passed in a surreal blur. At times I even noticed things I never knew were there, like an old farm, vintage road signs, and decrepit homes abandoned long ago.

I gripped Cam's hips tighter as all the constraints that held me down started to disappear. As the bitter chill whipped all around us, something that went beyond the frigid temperatures rattled my spine. I looked back over my shoulder, half expecting to see some boogeyman chasing us. Nothing was there. I turned back around and tried to refocus on Cam. But I just could not shake the feeling that something sinister was brewing.

Chapter Fifteen

Cam whisked me away to Shandaken, a rural town in Upstate New York. Nestled in a valley, it was a homespun community that was proudly devoid of any pretention. A few steeple-topped chapels and a small yet traditional downtown added to its country charm. If I did not know better, I would swear that Shandaken was not in the same state, let alone on the same planet, as New York City.

We pulled up to a rustic café right at the foot of a mammoth hill. Cam parked right in front, giving his gears a final rev. He then slid off the bike and held his gloved hand out to me. My legs buckled from the long drive, and my dismount was tipsy. But Cam supported my every move. The broad smile across his face told me that he was in his element. His normally intense demeanor was now relaxed and playfully easygoing. He was happy. And if Cameron Sterling was happy, I was happy for him.

"Maybe you wouldn't be so wobbly if you had some food in you," he jested.

"Maybe if someone fed me in the first place," I said, looking around. "But I can't fault you for bringing me here. This place is beyond words. How'd you find it?"

"I have a cabin not far from here. I bought it as an escape from the world."

"Wow, your own little fuck pad. If those walls could talk."

"They would have no gossip to tell. I've never had a guest up there."

"And tomorrow morning what will those walls say?"

Cam came closer to me. He took both my hands and kissed them while keeping me steady in his dark gaze. "You can't even imagine."

≈

Lilly and I had just finished dinner. I made sure we got the best table in the café. As we watched the dusk roll over the majestic snow-covered forest through a gigantic picture window, we clicked glasses of wine. A moose head was mounted on the wall right over Lilly's head. If it had been a different woman, the effect would have been comical. But the way the candlelit flickered about Lilly's face, that moose head just added to her mystique.

I noticed that Lilly had dropped that fake accent. She did not realize that she had slipped into her native tongue during our free-flowing conversation; there was no doubt she was from Southern California. With the disappearance of her front, her tone was light and breezy. I marveled in the naturalness of this woman as she moved her hands with excitement while she discussed the most mundane events and rolled her eyes to playfully exaggerate points. I could not help but smile as I was transported to some unknown beach, smelling the sea breeze and squeezing sand between my toes. I dared not mention any of this to Lilly for fear she would revert to that generic way of talking and break the spell.

After dinner Lilly and I walked hand in hand under the

shroud of night. The crystal-clear sky permitted the stars to brilliantly illume our path. We made it to the opening of a covered bridge. Lilly nuzzled up close to me as the wind circled around us lightly. Despite the romantic ambiance, she was indeed a city girl, jumpy at any crunch or crackle coming from the darkness of the surrounding woods. Her eyes darted about, searching for any signs of animal predators.

"Is it safe to be out here? What about mountain lions?"

"There are no wild mountain lions in New York. Now pythons, that's a different story."

Lilly almost jumped into my arms. "What?" She wrapped one leg around my thigh and was holding me like a life preserver.

"I'm just messing with you," I said.

"That's not funny," Lilly said as she slid her warm leg off me. I did not want her body to leave mine. I started toward her pink, pouty lips. But Lilly pulled away and turned her head. The darkness of the night hid her face from me. Even though I knew she was not trying to be difficult, I could not figure out what was going on in her head.

"What is it? Are you still scared?" I asked. I turned Lilly's face toward mine. Her eyes were glistening with tears. "What's wrong, baby?"

Lilly inhaled deeply and held her breath for a few seconds as though she was trying to keep something down. Then a rush of air blew out of her mouth, and before she could stop herself, Lilly let go. "There are some things about my past you don't know. I'm not the person you think I am."

I thought back to my dinner with Sig. Is this what he was talking about?

Lilly continued, "I think you see me as some effervescent socialite who the world bows down to. But there is more to me than that. I have my faults and have made more mistakes than I can count. And I have a secret. One that has kept me chained on the edge of a cliff, just dangling over a raging ocean. I've never told anyone, but it has eaten me up inside. And now you've come into my life—Mr. Perfect. I don't think I can measure up to you, and I'm terrified. When you find out how truly damaged I am, you'll disappear."

I took Lilly into my arms, where she went somewhat limp. As I propped her against my chest, I knew I had to make a decision. I could either take advantage of her vulnerable state tonight and abandon her at her house when I was done the next day. Or I could do what my heart compelled: give her compassion and understanding.

In a way I was just as damaged as Lilly, and I wished someone would have given me the same consideration. With a tinge of my own sadness, I said, "I won't judge you, and I won't disappear. But you can't keep running away from your problems. I will help in whatever way I can. However, you have to promise me that whatever you have been doing to cope, you have to stop it because it is not working. It is keeping you tethered to the very thing that is destroying you. Do you promise me?"

Lilly looked up at me with renewed hope. "I promise."

Maybe it was the night's air, or it could have been a new sense of connectedness caused by her vulnerability, but right then Lilly was utterly magnetic. My body fused to hers like she was the other half of me.

"Stay with me tonight," I beckoned. I gave her a soft kiss

on her neck to let her know I was not in it just for the sex. I wanted to satisfy not only her body but her mind and soul as well. Suddenly I was overcome by the desire to kiss her. The hot vapor of our breaths wafted up in hazy streams as mouths met in a dizzying kiss. My tongue hungrily searched for hers, and my cheeks puckered in deep as I sucked hard on it.

Lilly took her hand and grabbed my engorged dick, sending raging fire through it. I was as thick and long as the tall pines that surrounded us. My heart rate quickened as she stroked my member with delicate conviction. She took her other hand and meandered to my balls, alternating between kneading and finger flicks.

I picked Lilly up, and she wrapped her legs around my waist. I was so excited I nearly rammed her as I backed her into a tree. But I slowed the momentum down enough to just give her a thump. The only thing I wanted was to get my cock inside her as our hands went wild over each other's bodies.

"Right here. Right now," I said, just barely dry humping her. My hips pushed harder into hers. "I will fuck you right here."

From somewhere in the woods, an animal howled, and then there was the crunch of leaves under *something's* feet.

Lilly pushed me off her. "Do me here? I don't think so."

If I had any chance of getting me some woodland pussy, it was out of the question now. Smokey the Bear had seen to that.

The ride was short to Cam's mountain hideaway. As soon as we entered, Cam pulled me through the darkness of the living room. He turned on a small lamp with a dull bulb that was about to extinguish at any moment.

"Have a seat while I start the fire," he said.

"I thought you already did that," I said as I sat and coyly spread my legs. As Cam lit the fireplace, I looked around the room. It was a traditional log cabin filled to the brim with hunting trophies, handmade furniture, and a furry rug right in front of the fireplace.

How corny. But it works for me.

I got up and went to Cam's bookcase. *The Republic*, *Scientific Farm Animal Production*, *Smith and Roberson's Business Law*, and a hefty collection of *The Boondocks*. Cam most certainly was eclectic if nothing else. I then turned my attention back to him. His darkened silhouette stood against the blazing fire—long, lean, serpentine. He turned and strode toward me full of power and vigor. I trembled as goose bumps erupted through my skin. But he stopped before he reached me.

"Take off your clothes," Cam said with authority. Tonight he was the boss and wanted to be a voyeur. I loved it when he took control; that drove me absolutely wild. I was willing to do anything he asked.

"Whatever you want," I said.

"Don't talk unless I tell you to."

I did as I was told and wondered what was next. Was Cam just going to *take* me? I moved my hand to my zipper and slowly brought it down. I had not worn any panties, so the top of my shaved pubes greeted him. Cam licked his lips and nodded his head, an order for me to continue. The boots were next. I sat on a large chair and vampishly bent over. I untied my boots at an excruciatingly slow speed. I saw Cam's rock-hard dick pointed straight at me, long and thick.

As I kicked the boots off, I aimed them at Cam. I was being naughty and trying to get in trouble. He shook his head and said, "You don't want to do that. I'll have to spank you. And I will leave you red and raw."

I shyly put my finger on the side of my mouth and gave him a "who, me?" look. I pulled off my jeans and spread my legs wide. Cam's eyes squinted as he honed in on my love box. I then plunged two fingers all the way inside me and started thrusting them. I could see Cam's shoulders heaving from his deep breaths, growing progressively more bothered.

As my juices flowed more, sloshing sounds accompanied each probe of the masturbatory finger fuck. It was not only the masturbation making me hot. It was how Cam was looking at me—the way he was so intently focused on my throbbing pussy. He was consumed with it. Though he was in the prime power position, I was getting off on the tiniest bit of power I held at that moment. The power to totally captivate and mesmerize another human being.

Cam could see that I was about to shatter myself with an orgasm. But he was not having that. He marched over and pulled my fingers out of my pussy. He then sucked the nectar off them. I was taken aback by the gusto he cleaned my fingertips with. When Cam was done, he promptly yanked off my sweater. Not bothering to unclasp the bra, he pulled down one of the lacy cups and bit down on my nipple. It hurt like hell. I collapsed deeper into the chair, overwhelmed by ecstasy and pain, weighted down by Cam's massive dick resting on my fleshy pussy and stomach.

"Just do it already," I begged.

"Not on your terms but mine."

Cam turned me around so that my belly was on the chair. My ass was exposed, and he slapped it incredibly hard a few times. I screamed with joyous agony as the sting sent pricks throughout the rest of my body. Cam relished the way he could see my cunt from the back in this doggie-style position.

I suddenly got nervous. This was the way Sig did it, always from the back. I started to look back and ask Cam if we could do it some other way, but he moved my head back to the forward position. He thrust that dick into me with full power. I gasped as Cam's tip hit a spot deep inside my honey pot. This had never happened with Sig. What was going on?

As Cam pounded harder, waves of pleasure rippled through me. It felt so good that the moans stifled in my mouth. At the same time I felt a rush of fear surge through me. I mean it felt so fucking good; something just had to be wrong. I never gave credence to spontaneous combustion, but, Christ almighty, he was wreaking havoc with my pussy big time. Cam just kept on ramming with such confidence in his skills to take me there. Like a feline in heat, I arched my back and met him thrust for thrust. My wine flowed out of my goblet, cascading out of me and flowing down my inner thigh in a single creamy line.

Cam leaned forward and pinched my nipple. His other hand found my clit. He squeezed and rubbed both until they were raw. It hurt like hell, but he knew that mixing agony with delight would overload my pleasure circuits. And it did. Cam kept me pinned down and was not giving me any leeway to assert myself, making sure I knew I was his submissive. Fully in control, he continued to dive deep into my inner realm. My pussy tightened around his gigantic cock as I felt a sudden urge to bear down around it. I was thankful we were in the woods because of the stupendously loud moans escaping from my mouth.

"Jesus, Cam, I'm...I'm...I'm cumming," I said as I came hard. In fact, I came so hard that my contractions pushed his dick right out of me. I collapsed to the floor, totally spent.

"Sorry," I apologized with a sheepish grin. Cam did not smile back. His face showed his determination to be satisfied.

"You may be done, but I'm not," Cam said. He then put my legs in an open position and stood on his knees in between. He took both my hands and wrapped them around his dick—which seemed to have grown inexplicably larger—then slid them up and down. It was still coated by the thick lubrication gifted from my cunt. I really did need two hands to handle that long, thick beast. I was prone on the floor, and, from above, it looked like a girthy pipe. It took much effort to traverse its awesome length. I was exhausted from the love that Cam had just given me and had to use the last bit of my energy to jerk him off. Hand over hand, I tugged up the shaft with alternating constricting and contracting movements. On the down strokes, I bottle-capped it with twisting movements. Cam steadied himself by placing his hands on my bent knees.

"You like that?" I asked, watching his head rear back a bit.

"Aw, shit, yeah. You're the best," Cam said. He rocked his body between my thighs in sync with my hand strokes. Then Cam let out a grunt as he bucked and seized. He drew in a breath through his clenched teeth. Like from a pressurized water hose, hot cum shot all over my chest and stomach—the milk of the gods. Cam's release seemed to go on forever and wore him out. He sprawled on my stomach, totally drained of his fluids. He was so wasted that he did not mind that he was lying in his own cum.

Nor did I care about the drying love juice cementing us together. I looked down at Cam and stroked the top of his head. I finally had the lover I could only previously dream about. If bliss could be manifest in the physical world, surely this was it. For that moment in time, I had no crazy past, and Sig did not exist. Cam and I were engulfed in a happiness that expanded the boundaries of earth, space, and time. I truly believed that all was right in the world, that nothing bad could ever happen again.

Boy, was I wrong.

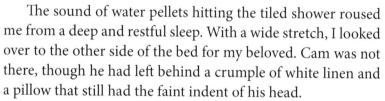

The sound of water pellets hitting the tiled shower roused me from a deep and restful sleep. With a wide stretch, I looked over to the other side of the bed for my beloved. Cam was not there, though he had left behind a crumple of white linen and a pillow that still had the faint indent of his head.

I found myself blushing and giggling as memories of the night's lovemaking came to mind. My hand stroked the folds and peaks where Cam's spectacular body had slumbered peacefully next to me. Wanting more, I leaned over and sniffed the scent he had marked the bed with. It was musky, mixed with his darkly scented cologne. I then happened to notice steam wafting from under the bathroom door like a dense fog rolling in. Propping myself up on my elbows, I stared at the door for a moment, contemplating whether or not to join him in the shower.

The light from Cam's phone broke my train of thought. The irritating call notification light kept blinking. Shit, that motherfucking phone had been receiving calls all night long. Cam tried to be discreet and not bring attention to it by putting the phone on mute at first, not wanting to turn it all the way off just in case the office called. But the phone just would not stop vibrating. Every time it did, Cam looked at it, and a severe frown would cross his face.

Now I was alone with Cam's phone. I really did not want to be nosy and violate his trust, but I did wonder why Wotherspoon and Associates would keep calling him in the wee hours of the night. Innocently, I picked up Cam's phone with every intention of not prying, just taking it to the bathroom and letting him deal with it. But as soon as I picked it up, a frosty shiver went down my spine. My alter ego suddenly woke up and prodded me to have a look-see.

I looked at the door and listened hard, making sure Cam was still showering. I swiped the phone's screen and saw that he had eighty-six missed calls and fifty-two texts. I swiped the screen again to see who was making these incessant calls. As I scrolled down, only one name popped up: Becky.

Who the fuck is fucking Becky? Okay, calm down. Becky must be a secretary or another lawyer at the firm. She needed to get in contact with Cam about a case. Yeah, that's what this shit right here is about.

That is what I told myself. But my alter ego materialized, smacking on gum and chewing on a toothpick at the same time. She told me that this whole situation reeked of donkey shit and that I had better get to the bottom of this Becky mess. I had to make it fast, though. The water from the shower had been cut off, which meant I only had a few minutes to read the texts. Of course, all of the texts were from Becky, and the last one said, "Fuck you." That was definitely not from a secretary or fellow coworker. I kept reading, and from what I could deduce, Cam had been in a longstanding relationship with Becky, and she wanted to know where the fuck he was.

I could not believe it. Cam was dicking around on me? Yeah, I had another man, but at least Cam knew about him. He was keeping this Becky bitch a secret. How shady was that? And she was not just some side piece; this was a relationship.

That asshole.

I hopped out of bed and marched over to the bathroom. I was so pissed that it did not even occur to me to put on some clothes. I thought about kicking the door open like I had seen on "Cops," but I was not about to break my foot. How would I explain that shit to Sig? I took a breath and opened the door as calmly as I could. But I was so stoked up with adrenaline that my hand was shaking. I boldly entered, mad-dogging my face. Cam threw me off guard when I saw his naked body glistening under the incandescent glare of the track lights.

"Hey, sexy lady. I see you finally decided to wake up," he said, none the wiser. He stood there all Adonis-like with that crooked smile. I gulped as I gawked at him pat drying his smooth, olive skin. I actually had to make myself remember why I was in there in the first place and refocus on getting into his ass. I thrust the phone in front of me.

"What the shit is this, Cam?"

"A phone," he responded, halfway confused and halfway snarky.

"Yeah, I know that motherfucking shit." I swiped the phone

and showed him the detailed account of texts and calls from Becky. "Who the hell is Becky?"

I went on a major tirade, spewing accusations like a lunatic. Cam did not belittle himself to join my whirlwind of volatile emotion. I wanted a response. Anything. A yell. Some curse words. Even a smack. I was used to those and knew how to deal with them. Silence was something I was ill equipped to handle. I just kept on screaming at Cam, trying to get some reaction out of him, and I finally did. He reached the limits of his tolerance and snatched his phone from me. Glaring, Cam said, "Let's not even get into why you are fucking with my phone, invading my privacy."

"Seriously! I just caught you and your nasty-ass girlfriend. And you have the nerve to talk to me about privacy. How long have you been involved with her?" My alter ego was cheering me on as she was air boxing.

"No, no, it's not about that, Lilly. The fact that you have the gall to come in here and go off on me is the problem. It did not cross your mind to ask me about it first. You just jumped to conclusions and came in here with guns blazing. I don't need this from you. I thought you left that shit at Sig's house."

Cam retained his dignity by putting on some boxers and returning to his self-possessed way of being. He walked right past me, refusing to stoop to my infantile level. I, on the other hand, was not done yet and was not about to let him get away without an explanation. I grabbed Cam by his arm. He looked down at his arm, up at my face, and then back down to his arm like I had lost my ever-loving mind. And I had.

Fuck that. Cam is not going to pull some kind of mind-fuck shit on me. Not today, buddy.

"Let me go," Cam snarled through his teeth.

"No, Cam. You will tell me who she is. I have a right to know."

He shook my hand off his arm. I trailed behind him as he went to his drawer for a sweater and a pair of jeans. Cam looked at me with what my alter ego registered as disgust.

"Look at you," he said. "You look ridiculous, standing there butt naked, arguing about some messages on *my* phone. A phone you had no business looking at in the first place."

I must admit I did look rather silly, all riled up in the middle of a log cabin with no clothes on. I was trying to put Cam on the spot when, in reality, I put myself in the vulnerable position. I tried to save face by putting my hands on my hips as if I did not care. "Don't change the subject, Cam. Who is she?"

Cam tossed one of his shirts at me. "Get dressed. As for Becky, I really don't owe you an explanation—especially in light of your childish behavior. But I'll tell you anyway. Becky… yeah, I've known her for a while. She was just someone I hung out with."

"Someone you fucked."

"Yeah, most definitely. I fucked her. I fucked her a lot. It was purely sexual. I had no real feelings for her."

"I read the texts, Cam. It was not just sex."

"Not to her. For me it was just a thing. That's why I haven't mentioned Becky. She was never that important to me. Not now, not ever. The only woman I cared about was you. And now look at us. I thought you and I had something special here. But you are showing me a side of you I did not know existed. And I don't like it."

Suddenly I could not breathe. This was that moment I was

dreading. That moment of rejection like I had gone through so many times before. I could feel a panic attack coming on. I did not want to take the drugs. However, if I did not get some Xanax in me, I was going to have a nervous breakdown right in front of Cam. If that happened there would be no chance of recovery. He would be gone forever.

I rushed over to my purse and swiftly took out a couple of Xanax. I gulped them down while Cam watched in shock for a few seconds. Then he stormed over to my purse and spilled its contents on the bed. He surveyed the pharmacy of prescription drugs it had hidden inside.

"Sig told me you had some issues, but I thought you were over it," he said, disheartened.

I dropped my head in shame, not knowing how to explain my angst to him. I did not expect someone as strong as Cameron Sterling to understand. He just shook his head as he processed the discovery he made about me. However, the disappointed expression on his face softened. It was being morphed by compassion.

Cam picked up a bottle of Xanax. "Is this who you think you are? Is this who you want to be?"

"No. I've tried so hard to shake it. But I can't get it out of my mind." I put my head in my hands to hide from Cam. There was no makeup, high fashion, or façade I could disappear behind. I could not bear for him to see the damaged essence of the real me.

Cam gently turned my face toward his. "I know you believe that there is something intrinsically wrong with you. But that is not true. This hurt woman is not who you really are—scared, acting out the only way she can. I look into your eyes and see the same look that I saw in my mother's eyes. She could have wound up like you if she had not been killed. Tell me who hurt you so badly. Who stole your joy?"

I did not want to tell Cam the truth. I did not want to hear it myself. But I could not stop the purge my emotional stomach vomited. "My dad…he did it. He had a thing for children, a preference, you could say. He indulged in his sickness for years before I was born. He did not pursue me at first. I guess he didn't want to shit where he slept. He was content with molesting other people's kids. Instead he abused me in other ways. Anything he could get his hands on—belts, extension cords, hot irons, bricks, you name it. I knew that was just a weird way for him to sublimate his repressed sexual desire for me and that one day he would come after me for real."

I could see the normally collected Cam squirm ever so slightly as I recounted my life to him.

Taking a cleansing breath, I said, "When puberty hit, that's when things changed. He finally made his move in the middle of a summer night. I fought him off the best I could. I had to. I know she heard the commotion coming from my room, but my mother was pathetic. I'm not blaming her. At this point she had been beaten down by my father physically and spiritually. That day, when I rebuffed dad's advances, he knew he could not have me like that. He decided to inflict more terror upon me, thereby ensuring I would never tell anyone our secret. After the attack, he hung me out of a window and threatened that if I ever told anyone, he would kill my mother. I was mad at Mom for not sticking up for me, but I did not want to see her harmed. I kept my mouth shut.

"Then the drugs came. I did it all thinking they were some

kind of saviors. I'd try anything to make me forget how my father looked at me…that lustful look in his eyes. I believed his declaration that I was nothing and that no one would ever want me in *that way* except him. It took a lot of drugs to cloud Father's words, and I ended up in rehab. The best thing really. I got clean and entered a couple of modeling competitions. I was applauded for my looks, and I liked it. I left California as fast as I could. I dropped anything in my personality that connected me to California and became reborn. But you can never escape your history, not really, not ever. So the person you know, the one that everyone knows, was born out of pain."

Cam had to take a seat. He was straight and stiff as a board. I understood that he had to prop himself up from all that heaviness I just laid on him. He took a contemplative breath and said, "She—the person you're pretending to be—is not you. You have to reclaim yourself, but you can't do it with those pills. They are not doing anything except keeping you trapped in the past, giving you a false impression of freedom. I know it hurts. I've felt that kind of pain myself. But you went to that memorial with me and helped me face it. And I will do the same for you. I'm here and will do whatever it takes to help you overcome these demons. However, it is ultimately up to you. You have got to want to be better. You have got to want to be strong. You have got to believe in yourself. I can't and will not do that for you. Am I understood?"

I broke down in response to Cam's words. I knew I could no longer tread the treacherous path I had been stumbling along. At the end of that path was death either through drugs or suicide, and I knew it. I curled up in a mass of tears on the bed, ashamed at being exposed and confused as to what to do next. But even though I was blubbering, I somehow felt a little bit better.

Cam graciously spooned up behind me. His strong arms embraced my trembling body as he pulled me closer to his warm skin. I started to settle down as I closed my eyes with relief. His warm breath blowing across the back of my neck lovingly caressed me. I finally felt a sense of safety that I had never experienced before.

Chapter Sixteen

After that rocky morning, Cam and I spent two more days at the cabin. He bought me some clothes and cleared some space in a drawer and closet for me. We walked the trails, and he taught me about nature, which helped me overcome some of my fear about the woods. Cam turned out to be a pretty good cook as he indulged my taste buds with fine Italian cuisine. Nights were spent making love and falling asleep in each other's arms.

We were now on our way back home since Sig's flight would be arriving later on that night. Cam drove slowly, way under the speed limit. He was in no hurry to get me back. Neither was I. I sat on the back of the motorcycle, hoping it would transform into some sort of time machine that would transport us back to a few days earlier.

Unfortunately, we started our final approach to the destination. It was desolate and creepy out on the main road that was perpendicular to Sig's driveway. Cam and I appeared to be the only two living creatures around. However, I did notice some strange car parked on the shoulder. As we drove past, I looked at the car. There was no driver, and the hazard lights were not flashing.

Where did the driver go? We didn't pass anyone coming up. And there is nothing at the other end of the road. Hmmm.

I was about to point out the obvious car to Cam. However,

as soon as he drove us to the entrance of the property, my mind went blank with dread. Cam's bike grumbled toward the opulent mansion that might as well have been a carnival spook house. It looked so dark and drab. A sense of impending doom descended upon me. I squeezed Cam tighter as he parked the bike. We sat there for a few moments with me still clutching him.

"I don't want you to go either, but Sig is on his way," Cam said.

Hesitating, I let Cam go, and he assisted me off the bike. I mournfully sighed as I strapped my helmet back in place.

"Well, I guess this is it. I wish it didn't have to be this way," I said while holding back tears.

"For now it's the only way," Cam said, taking my hands. "When can I see you again?"

I stared deeply into his eyes, those gorgeous mahogany pools. I wanted to swim and float in them. "I don't know."

Cam suddenly grabbed me and gave me an earth-shattering kiss. But I heard the chime of the grandfather clock from inside the house. It was like a harbinger for the wickedness returning. Cam released our intertwined fingers.

Hurriedly, I went inside, not daring to look back. If I had, I would have left with Cam. I opened that door as fast as I could before I changed my mind. Cam sensed my ambivalence and waited for me to come back. When he saw that I was not going to do that, he made sure I was safe and then got on his bike. I peeked out the window and watched Cam drive away, all my joy leaving with him.

Little did I know that there was a spy hidden in a dense thicket of trees. It was Jacob, and he had been videotaping Cam and me. A sinister smile crossed his face as Cam unknowingly drove past him, headed to the main road. Unbeknownst to Cam, he passed that peculiar car—Jacob's car—parked on the road's shoulder. He did not even give it a second thought.

As for me, I turned on all the lights in the house in a fruitless effort to ease my soul. I looked around at the penitentiary I was sentenced to, surrounded by all its invisible bars and specter guards. I was about to trudge upstairs to the bedroom, the main cell block, but caught a glance of Sig's monstrous portrait instead. Possessed by an avenging spirit, I spontaneously pulled a pair of scissors from a hall desk and stabbed at the portrait like I was reenacting the shower scene in *Psycho*. Hysterical delight enveloped me as I ran the blades straight down the portrait. I stood there laughing like a madwoman… until I realized what I had done.

Shit. How the fuck am I going to explain this? Sig's ten-thousand-dollar painting ripped to shreds. He is most certainly going to take that out on my ass.

If that happened, I could not call Cam and ask for his help. That would just give him an excuse to fuck Sig up, and then he would be in true danger. I had to deal with this on my own. I figured I would just lie like I always did with Sig, tell him I accidently knocked the painting down or some other ridiculousness. I might get slapped around some, but I could handle that.

I wondered why I continued living this way. Why didn't I stand up for myself and walk out that door? The reasons went beyond the typical excuses battered wives and girlfriends give. All of my reasons led to one place: my father. I knew that my relationship with Sig had its roots with my father, and until I reconciled that, I would not be strong enough to leave, and even if I did, my life would still be fucked up.

The only thing left to do was go upstairs and let some water run over my body to relieve the tension that was ratcheting up inside of me. Besides, I had Cam's spice all over me. I decided against a shower in favor of a bath; I had too much of Cam *on and in* me for a mere shower to remove. As I undressed, I noticed that I had no desire to take any of my prescriptions. Actually I felt surprisingly serene.

I stepped into the steamy bath with the expectancy that things would go well between Sig and me. Maybe tonight when he got home, we could have a civilized conversation, maybe even some genuine levity. Hope *almost* sprang eternal.

"Get up, you filthy tramp."

I thought I was dreaming when I heard those words. That is why I did not open my sleeping eyes right away. But they snapped open as soon as I was yanked out of bed and thrown on the floor. That is when I realized that what was going on was real. I was totally disoriented, startled from a dead sleep to being the victim of a full-on attack.

When my eyes finally focused, I saw that my brutalizer was Sig. I swear his eyes were red like Satan's. He stood over me holding a chunk of my hair in his hand.

"What are you doing?" I said like a fool, expecting a rational response.

Sig squatted over me and played a video on his phone. It was footage of Cam and me kissing. The first scene featured video of when Cam picked me up and the rest when he dropped me off. I was amazed that someone was so close to me, filming my every move. It was more disturbing that I did not even notice that they were there. Talk about a violation.

"It's not what you think," I said. I know that was lame to say, but it was the first thing to pop into my mind. Sig was not buying it.

"Out of all the men you could have fucked around with, you had to choose Cameron Sterling. You know what I said I would do if I found out who your lover was."

"Do whatever you want to me but please don't hurt him," I begged.

Sig stepped over to the side, and I saw the shadows of two other men in the room.

"Gentlemen, please come forward," Sig instructed.

Out of the darkness the two sinister males emerged. Sig introduced them. At the time I had absolutely no idea who either of these men were, but they were introduced to me as Chief Pepperdine and Xander, no last name.

"Seeing you down on the floor, begging for Cam's life, has made me realize something about my initial promise," Sig said.

"Your initial threat, you mean," I said defiantly.

"No, no, no. You should know me well enough by now to know that I don't make threats. I only make promises. But promises were meant to be broken. And I am breaking the one I made you. Well, sort of. See, I can look at you and tell that killing him would bring me no satisfaction. However, what will bring me pure delight is seeing you suffer. And the most suffering I can give you is the knowledge that Cam is still alive, and you can never have anything else to do with him. You will have to live with the fact that he will move on, meet another woman, possibly settle down and live a very happy life. You, however, will be with me…forever my worthless whore. And you want to know how I know this?"

Sig motioned Xander over with a pair of pliers and a little container of acid. From the look on his face, Xander was stoked; he wanted to hurt me. I jumped up and tried run away, but Xander knocked me right back to the floor. He held my arms down at my sides with his knees. I tried to kick my way from under him, but he was just too heavy. Xander proceeded to force my mouth open and plunged the pliers in. My heart felt like it was going to explode as sheer panic overwhelmed me.

I tried my best to escape by thrashing about like a fish on a shore as Xander started to pull my molar. The pain was so excruciating that I almost blacked out. Xander's lips curled back tautly into a closed-mouth smile. Even with that grin he was the most terrifying man I had ever seen. This was because his eyes did not crinkle or narrow when he smiled and were void of any emotion except desire to inflict as much pain as possible.

Xander was not the only one having a good time. A wicked smile found its way onto Sig's face too. "That's how I know you'll be with me forever. You know that if you try to leave… well, let's just say if you think the pliers are painful, just wait until that acid hits you."

Sig pointed at Chief Pepperdine, who was holding an elastor tool—what they use to castrate bulls. He said, "Now, if you do not stop seeing Mr. Sterling and gladly accept your position as my property, Cam will be clipped. No anesthetic, no chaser. If a neutered lover is not enough to keep you away *then* I will have to have Cam killed, but not before he is skinned first. See, you ignorant trollop, you cannot win this game. You have nowhere to run, nowhere to hide. I have got a team of people to shut you down. Once something belongs to me, it always belongs to me. That means you. Xander, you can stop pulling now."

Xander was disappointed that Sig would not let him finish ripping out my tooth. Before he took the pliers out of my mouth, he made sure to push them to the back of my throat. Sadistic shithole. He got off of me, leaving me to writhe in pain, choking and holding my throat.

Sig dismissed the men and stood next to me. "So you understand your place, or do you need more lessons?"

"I get it, Sig. Fuck, I get it."

"No more Cam?"

I relented. "No more. I'm done with him. Just leave him be." I did not dare to look at Sig, afraid that I would see the devil himself standing in front of me. Sig was right about one thing. It was worse to know that Cam was safe and that I could never see him again rather than dead. I know that was a morbid and selfish thought, but it was true. At least with death there is finality. However, if what you want is simply out of reach or taken away, that is torture.

Sig pursed his lips and released a long breath like he was dragging on a cigarette after a good nut. Torturing me actually gave him an orgasmic charge. Sick fuck. He started out of the bedroom to join his evil colleagues but turned back.

"By the way, what happened to my portrait?" he asked, surprisingly with not that much concern in his voice. He observed me holding my cheek as I tried to put pressure on my tooth to stop the throbbing. Sig grinned with pride. "Oh, who cares? I can get another painting anytime. That is a benefit of having money. You can buy whatever or whoever you want. I bought you right out of the bargain bin."

I got off the floor and rubbed my arms where Xander dug his knee into them. The pain from my tooth caused me to see stars as I stumbled into the bathroom. I thought about jumping out of the window to escape but looked down toward the driveway and saw Sig, Chief Pepperdine, and Xander. That is when I knew I had no place to go. I dared not bring Cam into this mess any more than he was already in it. Sig would come through on his "promises" regarding Cam's punishment.

I certainly was not going to involve Tamara. She was a good friend and deserved to be impervious to my bullshit. I had no money of my own, not even credit cards or bank accounts in my name. I had to get strong enough to leave this mayhem behind. Besides, even if Sig did not exist, there would be no way I could be with Cam as long as I remained as fucked up in the head as I was.

Somehow I had to commit murder. I had to kill my alter ego. But she was a tricky bitch. She had perfect hiding places and knew the ideal times to attack me. She knew my every weakness and what I was most afraid of. My alter ego was best buddies with my father. He groomed her, showed her how to rule me. They conspired against me in tandem and were a perfect team. It was my alter ego that chose Sig, not me. She picked him because he was so much like my father. She knew he would pick up where my father left off. That is why I was so weak and pathetic around him. That is why he could do what the fuck he wanted to. My alter ego told me that I would be nothing more than Sig's slave and that I might as well take those pills to at least feel better about it.

I did not listen to my alter ego this time. I flushed all the pills down the toilet instead.

Chapter Seventeen

I sat at the window listening to the pattering of raindrops against the pane. The morose droplets mimicked the tears streaming down my face. I wiped my eyes as my blurred vision tricked me into seeing a fading mirage of Cam across the yard. The woe of a bitter chill raced through me as his phantom image totally disappeared into the wispy haze. I closed my heavy sweater around me, crawling into a cable-knit shell and wishing Cam was cradling me instead.

An epic battle between my mind and soul had taken its toll on me. This was because Cam had been calling and texting me all week. I ignored the communication, which was about as easy as walking on glass. I had to let the love of my life go. Every time I thought about it, I could sense a panic attack coming on.

Though the mirage had dissipated, Cam's presence still hung heavy in the room—a revenant composed of all the life-giving oxygen I breathed in. With every inhale, my lungs burned from the searing remembrance of that man. The more breaths I took, the more the fire engulfed me. The point came where I found myself gasping as I begged to hit the bottom of the blazing bottomless pit I had been plunged into.

The pills? Yes, I still had a secret stash in the house. These were the ones my alter ego would not let me throw away. When the agony of my separation from Cam became almost too much to bear, I nearly succumbed. That scenario played out nearly twenty-four hours a day, almost nonstop temptation.

I even contemplated suicide, but what good would that have done? While I would be rotting in my grave, the whole world would rally around Sig. That monster would become a martyr who sacrificed his pure, undying love to the selfish, weak bitch who killed herself over nothing. But it would not have been over nothing; it would have been because I lost my life before destroying my body. And that life was Cam.

Forcing Cam out of my life did not make me weak; it was a testament to my burgeoning strength. However, the separation had made me sick. A Herxheimer reaction was destroying and building me back up. Though this alchemy felt like it was killing me, it indeed had a purpose. That purpose, in the end, would make me stronger because I had to unselfishly give Cam up to save his life. No, that did absolutely nothing to lessen the pain. But it gave me solace to know that at least Cam would be protected.

Still, I wish that I had the chance to explain to Cam the reasons for my actions. Of course it was more than a little shitty leaving things the way I did. I wanted to call and tell him that I was not angry at him, that I had not had a change of heart, that I adored him. But fast-forwarding to a grim outcome, I accepted that maybe we just were not meant to be. I prayed that Cam would come to understand the seemingly cruel way I cut off all ties with him. The last thing in the world I wanted to do was make him feel the rejection that I had felt my entire life.

But Sig was insane and made it clear what the repercussions would be if I continued seeing Cam.

I actually had to propel my body off the window seat

because it was drained by all the emotional drama that had transpired. I lumbered over to the remote control and turned on the television for a much-needed distraction from heartbreak. Collapsing onto the studded leather couch, I felt like a bowling bowl dropping on cement. Though Sig purchased that couch years earlier, it was still hard and stiff. It was his favorite piece of furniture in the entire house—hard and unyielding just like him.

Flipping aimlessly through channels, I passed one that had my entire face superimposed on the screen. *What in the shit is going on?*

Needless to say, I stopped on that channel and turned up the volume to see what the deal was. A gushy piano soundtrack overlaid a montage of shots featuring Sig and me fake-posing for photographers, pretending to be a happy couple. The last shot featured a photo of our trip to St. Tropez. Sig was kissing me on the cheek, and I was flashing a toothy grin. However, it was a farce, as usual. On that same supposed romantic getaway, Sig and I did not even share bedrooms. Fuck, we were on different floors of the hotel. And that kiss that everyone cooed over? Well, Sig struggled to even put his lip skin on my face, and when the photographers left, he promptly wiped it off with sanitizer.

The tabloid news reporter informed the viewing audience about how Klå stock had quadrupled since I had become Sig's girlfriend and that he was now a billionaire. She remarked that I was his good luck charm.

So that was it…the reason Sig did not see to it that I was disfigured or Cam was killed. That slime ball was protecting his investment, keeping an eye on the bottom line. He knew the whole time that I was the reason not only for some of his success…hell, I was the reason for all of it. As long as the prospect of Cam getting killed was an option, Sig could manipulate me however he wanted to.

Sig came downstairs dressed in an expensive royal blue suit. It made him look deader than he normally did. He paused for a moment and just stared at me. He was evaluating my value to him and if it was even worth it to keep me alive. I could see his facial muscles tighten as he went back and forth about what to do with me. After a long while, Sig made up his mind. He abruptly thrust a long-sleeved dress at me and tossed some pumps over to my feet. The outfit matched his in color. "Put this on. We have a meeting with Mr. Wotherspoon today," he said dryly.

I assumed that Cam would not be at this meeting. After all, Sig's plan was to keep us apart.

"Why should I go? Are you planning on having me jumped or lynched today?" I asked, totally feeling my Wheaties.

Sig headed in my direction. He displayed his dominance by standing over me. I turned my face away from him, not wanting to expose my distress. I trained my eyes on the television that was still showing my face with a scroll of the millions of dollars Sig had earned in the past year from clothing, fragrances, and an upcoming beauty line.

The next thing I knew Sig jerked me up from the couch by my shoulders. For such an angular man, he had a tremendous amount of strength to call upon whenever he was angered. He stood me squarely in front of him as he dug his long, pointy nails into my skin. I flinched and reared back at the coldness of his sandpaper touch.

"Why would I do that to a lovely creature such as you? Though it is business, I am merely offering an invitation for an afternoon out. Ever since you met Chief Pepperdine and Xander, you have been out of sorts," Sig said in his sarcastic yet psychotic way.

Really, you have the gall to say I am out of sorts. Those assholes threatened me with acid and tried to rip out my teeth.

Sig said, "I know you want to pout. But, really, what good is that going to do you? Absolutely none. Your life can be so easy if you only cooperate. I have given you the world. The least you can do is act with a bit of gratitude. You can oblige me that much, can't you?"

I tried to disassociate as Sig's nails became daggers puncturing my skin. I could feel them burrowing down to muscle.

"No disrespect, but most gifts do not come with blood works. After meeting Xander, I am more than sane to ask what you have in store for me next. What is the meeting about? This meeting that seems to have fallen out of the ether and demands such immediacy," I said.

Oops. I had crossed the line with Sig once again by asserting my right to know and have some say-so about my life. I winced in pain as I started bleeding where he placed his clawed grip. I tried to run, but Sig had me trapped. With horror, I watched this hellion. He pursed his mouth into a tiny pucker as a barely discernable twitch enlivened his eye.

"I've already been merciful with you once. Do not test my patience. Just do as you are told," he said flatly. That moment confirmed that Sig had no soul in his body. He was just a vessel for the manifestation of evil.

I looked over Sig's shoulder to make sure Xander was not

lurking around. When I did not see the ominous shadow of his menacing form coming at me, I knew I was somewhat safe. This relative safety was threadbare and dependent on my cooperation with Sig. I did not want to give in to him. I wanted to jump on his scrawny ass and beat the shit out him. But he was standing there looking at me with my father's eyes. My fragile countenance fell as my alter ego took over. She told me I was trapped and to do as I was told. If I did not, she would make sure that I did something stupid that would not only hurt me but Cam also. I did not think that my fucking crazy ego would be so hard to defeat.

Since I was already down, my alter ego made a suggestion. She thought it would be proper if I begged Sig to let me see Cam again. Yes, I was that desperate. The rationale was that Sig was the gatekeeper that stood between us. There was no other barrier. If I begged enough, made myself look like a fool, then that would be enough to satisfy Sig's sadistic streak. I would allow him to bully, humiliate, and torture me as much as he wanted. But Sig had to give me something in return, and that was an opportunity to see Cam, no matter how brief.

"Can I at least tell Cam that I am sorry?" I meekly asked.

Quicker than a lightning strike, Sig grabbed me by the neck and ran me into the wall. He started choking me.

"What? Where did that come from? That request is so half-witted that I cannot fathom why you would bring it up," he said, banging my head against the wall. "I am trying to make your life better, and you bring him up."

I felt a blackout coming on. I had to distract him. "Sig, we'll be late for the meeting. I know you don't want any visible markings on me. So let's discuss this at a later time. I need time to get ready. I don't even have makeup on yet," I said, trying to appear like I was not scared shitless.

Sig did not immediately release my neck. With suspicion, he turned his head a bit while keeping both eyes on me. "See what you have done? Because you started an argument, we do not have enough time for you to properly dress. You will just have to put your makeup on in the car. Just put on the dress now."

I heard bells and whistles, like cartoonish blasts of smoke coming out of my ears. Something was definitely wrong. Sig was the most anal person I had ever come across. I swore sometimes that his middle name was Sphincter. So it was strange for him not to plan an event or meeting down to the minute details. This all sounded like he was being spontaneous, something he never, ever did.

Reluctantly, I took the dress with me into a half bath. There was no way I was going to balk in front of Sig; I did not want to have another encounter with Xander. I locked the door behind me to guard against any intruders then placed the dress over the toilet and immediately searched the bathroom like an inmate in prison. Really, that is what I was for all practical purposes. I needed a shank. But there was nothing in the bathroom except toilet paper, soap, and hand towels. I shook my head in defeat and promptly started to take off my clothes.

I held up the dress before I put it on. Under different circumstances I would have adored its handcrafted elegance. It was a cocktail dress but could easily be worn to any formal occasion. Its royal blue color made it spark with vibrancy. The fabric was cottony soft and smelled of the perfumed paper from the designer box it came out of. However, all of those things made no difference in light of the bizarre circumstance I was thrust into. I still could not shake the feeling that this would be the dress I would be buried in.

As I slipped the dress onto my body, I could not help but wonder what Sig had planned for me. He was diabolical and knew what he was doing by throwing me off guard. That was one of his many ways to disrupt my equilibrium and keep me mired in confusion and depression. Admittedly, Sig's method worked. My Stockholm syndrome was well set with my alter ego totally bonded with him.

I could barely zip the dress because of the mad thoughts infiltrating my head. This was how Sig inflicted mental torture on me even when he was not in the room. I was definitely trained. If Sig was not around, his training made me do fucked- up shit to myself. I made sure I remained his property and would continue to do whatever he wanted, whenever he wanted. Shit, that is how that motherfucker came up a winner each and every time.

This was a battle of wills, and right now I was fighting in the dark with my hands tied behind my back. Today the only way to combat Sig was to confront whatever surprise he had lined up for me. I decided that I would at least try to be brave. No matter what that sociopath had in store for me, I would face it. I looked in the mirror once more and wondered if that would be the last time I saw myself. I kissed my fingertips and then pressed them against my sad reflection—a little self-love come much too late.

Like my entire life with Sig, it was a stressful ride to The Plaza. I sat on the other side of the limousine from him with my arms folded and my knee pressed against the door. I did not want my body anywhere near his. If I could have ridden on the roof of that limousine, I would have.

Sig looked down at my knee with disgust. It was beet red and chafed from the pressure I put on it. "I have lost all tolerance and patience with you. I have had enough of your insolent pouting. You will put a smile on your face and represent me to the best of your ability. Otherwise Xander may have to pay you another visit."

I rolled my eyes and kept my face turned toward the window. I was trying to block out Sig's threat, but the thought of Xander gave me the shakes. To take my mind off Xander, I watched random people on the street going about their daily lives. These were the same people who envied my storied life so much. They fantasized about having my house, cars, money, and looks. They could not see the beauty in their own lives—lives that they believed to be so mundane or petty. I wished to God that I could switch places with them. At that moment, they had no idea how I prayed that same God would strike Sig down with a stroke, just severe enough to paralyze his mouth. But God was not with me, and Sig just kept at me.

"Look at you. With that frown on your face, you look like you are a hundred years old. Tomorrow we are going to a doctor and getting you some Botox and schedule a much-needed nip and tuck."

"Fuck you, Sig," I said.

The driver was looking back at us in the rearview mirror.

Though the partition was up and the driver could not hear our conversation, he could tell from Sig's facial expression and the way he was about to lurch at me that something was very wrong.

Sig saw the driver watching him and settled back into his seat. He said through his teeth, "I see you picked an opportune time to backtalk me. But let me give you a warning. Do not tread on me, for I am a formidable enemy. I will not hesitate to destroy the object of your desire. I would advise you to at least pretend that you are happy. You do not want your adoring fans to see you looking haggard on all the magazine covers and Internet blogs. Like Xander, they will rip you apart."

My shallow insecurity agreed with Sig. I remember once I went out on a casual errand with no makeup and schlumpy clothes. Some photographer caught me, and I was negative tabloid fodder for at least a month. Though I knew I had to work on myself, I could not conquer all my demons with a simple snap of my fingers. This difficult process would take time, and each little monster had to be defeated one by one. However, the little beast of vanity would have a victory today.

I pulled out my mirror and touched up my makeup, making sure to hide any bruises I received from Xander's blitz and Sig's choking. The evidence of Sig's abuse was minimal, nothing a little concealer around the neck could not handle. Thank goodness he did not choke me for that long. I then focused on the rest of my face. It was tremendously difficult to keep my lipstick from smearing as the limousine seemed to seek out every pothole and bump. But it was a welcome distraction from the pressure-cooker tension building up in the air. As I looked at my perfectly arched brow, I thought that the least Sig could have done was tell me I looked good. But that asshole sat there with that dour look on his aging face, his unwanted stare critiquing me.

Why do I care what Sig thinks about my looks? He sure as fuck does not give a shit what I think about his. If I did, I would tell him how he looks like the capital of the State of Ugly.

Sig could not be more barf inducing. I do not know how I did not see it before, but his jawline remarkably resembled my father's. I stared at him a little while longer as his face seemed to take on more of my father's features. Anxiety knotted up in my stomach, and I felt the need to search the limousine for a vomit bag. Right there in the backseat, Sig was transforming into my father. Thankfully, we arrived at The Plaza. As the limousine pulled up to the curb, Sig's true form came back. Never have I been so relieved to see his awful face. Sig scrutinized me with one final once-over.

"I guess that will have to do. There is not much we can do to correct the abomination called you," Sig said right before he exited the limo. I sat still and waited for him to at least offer his hand to me. No such luck. The driver saw my embarrassment. He promptly got out of the limousine and opened the door for me.

"If you will do me the honor, madam," the driver said as he extended his hand to me.

Sig immediately grabbed the limo driver's arm and spun him around. Unfortunately, the driver was not only a small man but one who avoided physical confrontations. Otherwise he probably would have popped Sig one.

"What do you think you are doing? She does not need your help. Get back in the car," Sig said to the driver. Man, he did not want anyone to help me.

Now, what the driver lacked in body size and aggression,

he made up for with knowledge of street psychology. Having been a driver for over a decade, he had come across so many people like Sig—entitled, arrogant assholes. He knew their secrets and lies. More than that, he knew what they feared the most. That fear was to be below someone else. They were pushed to be on top of the heap of humanity.

The driver shook off Sig's hand. "Sir, I assumed a man of your caliber would insist on only the finest treatment for his loved one. I would."

Even though the limo driver's barb was incredibly subtle, Sig understood that he just had his ass handed to him by what he considered to be a lowly person.

The driver offered his hand to me again. "May I assist you, please?" he respectfully and kindly asked. I tried not to laugh at Sig, who was standing there with his rage-filled eyes wide open. I took the driver's hand, and he gave me a friendly wink.

With a bit more confidence, I slid out of the limousine and slipped the driver a large tip. I approached the hotel's entrance and noticed that the doormen and concierge were extremely excited to see me. They all looked like they were in on some joke that was on me. I hesitated before walking into that hotel. I just knew that something shitty was waiting for me.

The concierge took Sig and me to the Terrace Room. There, we were greeted not only by Mr. Wotherspoon but carefully selected members of the firm, media, and major players in the fashion industry. Xander and Chief Pepperdine loomed nearby. The concierge had somehow come up from behind me like a ghost and, under the direction of Sig, took my purse.

"Hey, what are you doing?" I asked.

"Ms. Amsel, I assure you that your property will be properly looked after," the concierge said as he walked away.

"Sig, my purse."

"Quit your whining. Can't you see these people have been waiting for you?" Sig snapped under his breath.

Why do I suddenly feel like the last hamburger at a cookout? Okay, don't panic. Whatever you do, do not let them see you sweat.

I put on my counterfeit smile and leaned over to whisper in Sig's ear. "What is this all about?"

Sig just walked away without any explanation, leaving me there to deal with an onslaught of people converging around me. They offered me the usual compliments, but this time I was not filled up by them. Instead I felt smothered as my very breath was being robbed from me. As I tried to escape the vultures trying to eat pieces of me, I caught sight of Cam. He was standing off to the side by himself. His brow was furrowed as his eyes revealed how upset he was at me and the confusion that accompanied it.

Cam motioned to me with his head, making sure not to draw any unwanted attention to him or me. He wanted me to ditch the crowd and join him in a secluded spot. I looked over at Xander and Chief Pepperdine, who were keeping close watch over me. I could not let them see me silently communicating with Cam. I broke off contact and tried to pretend like I did not see him. I hated to do that to him, but I was not taking any chances with his life.

Sig went up to a podium and began to speak. I was not paying attention to anything emitting from that black hole he called his mouth until I heard him say, "Lilly, my love, could you please join me?"

The zestful crowd clapped as I awkwardly joined Sig on the stage. I kept glancing up, halfway expecting some pig's blood to fall from the ceiling. Instead, Sig put his arm around my waist. His touch was so repellent that I started to convulse a little bit. However, the crowd thought I was having a loving reaction toward Sig and let out a rapturous sigh.

Argh. Cue gag reflex.

"I know that the world has been straddling on needles, wondering who I would pick to be the new face of my company. It would have to be someone who embodied the style and innovation of the brand. Also, I am not beyond nepotism. Therefore, the choice was not difficult. Today I am announcing the new face of Klå—Lilly Amsel," Sig said to the enthralled audience.

My body went numb, and I became a mute. Something that resembled a smile plastered on my face, but it was really a high state of panic. I should have been happy. I had been coveting this position for the longest time, and now it made me want to shit my pants.

"But that is not all," Sig said as he removed a velvet box from his pocket. He dropped to one knee.

Oh, no, Sig. Don't do it. Please don't do it. Not here.

The room started to rapidly spin, yet I heard Sig's next words in slow motion. "Will you marry me?" He almost seemed sincere.

Though everyone else in the room thought Sig's proposal was a beautiful gesture, I knew it was really an order. He had orchestrated this whole drama. Not only did he come off like the most wonderful lover in the world, but he upped the ante by giving me the spokesmodel position. He knew that with all the press there I would not say no, that I would save face.

Damn my alter ego.

Still in shock, I started to swoon, and my head bobbled in such a way that it appeared that I had nodded in the affirmative.

What! No, wait. I didn't mean to do that. God, could you please reverse the rotation of the earth so we could start all over again? Fuck me. Where is Superman when you need him?

Suddenly there was a loud pop, and confetti fell like a storm under a circus tent. The crowd lost its mind and filled the room with cheering and clapping. Cam stood at the back of the room with his mouth agape. He watched with disbelief as Sig planted a weird smooch on my resisting lips. In that moment Sig and I turned into Michael Jackson and Lisa Marie sharing that horrendous VMA kiss. His lips released mine with the sound of a vacuum.

Sig turned to the crowd. "She said yes. Lilly Amsel is going to be my wife."

While Sig spoke to reporters, I waved them off as I tried to cork an impending bout of hyperventilation. If I had been stronger, I would have gone off on Sig right then and there. However, insecurity and the desire to keep up appearances made me keep it classy. I decided to let him down easy when we got home.

Amid all the well-wishers, I noticed that one person was not there. I looked around the room and only caught a fleeting glimpse of Cam's coattail as he disappeared out the door. I started to go after him when a heavy hand landed hard on my shoulder. I did not even have to turn around to see who it belonged to. That is because I recognized the hot breath that smelled like sewage, and it belonged to Xander. He swung me around so that I faced him and his stanky foot-sweat breath. He had seen Cam leave, too, and knew that I was going to follow him. Xander was an excellent enforcer and was not about to let that happen.

"I know why Sig is doing this. But you? Why are you doing it? You don't even know me. Do you have any sort of heart?" I asked Xander.

He just looked at me. He was void, totally blank. I was stunned that a human being could have absolutely no empathy for another.

Sig joined us. "Lilly, Xander is part of our family now. But he will only be called upon if I need him. Don't make me need him. Do you understand?" Sig said as he pulled Xander and me closer together.

Little did I know that while I was trapped with Sig and Xander, Chief Pepperdine was going through my purse and confiscated my cell phone.

Under the eagle eyes of Sig and Xander, I took a seat. Even though it was not the best, my life as I knew it had indeed ended. I was dead. Xander and Sig were the pallbearers. The blue dress truly was the one I was buried in.

Chapter Eighteen

"Well, Lilly. I guess you got one over on me. I didn't think anyone could do that, but you somehow managed to fuck me over. That's okay. It looks like you and Sig are a perfect match. He's an asshole. And you? Maybe birds of a feather... well, you know the rest. I hate to say this because it is hard for me, but I won't call you again. Really, what you did was beyond reproach. Despite that I want you to know that I did care for you deeply. And though you betrayed me, somehow I still wish you the best. Good-bye, Mrs. Krok."

That was the last message I left on Lilly's cell phone. Ever since Sig's proposal, I had been caught in a cyclone that had blown my heart hither and yon. I could hardly fathom that Lilly was actually going to marry another man. And out of all the men in the world she could have chosen, she picked Sig. Wow. That proved that she was one big mindfuck.

Thinking back, it was my screw-up, though. It was my mistake for trusting Lilly. I believed her lies, was entrapped by her beauty, and fell hard for all her deceptions. Shit, I don't even want to think about her pussy.

Sig was right about Lilly. She was the type of woman who never went backward when it came to the financial stature of her men. Sig had the cash and power. I was a mere lawyer, grasping at a partnership. Lilly played me against Sig; she must have been weighing her options the whole time. I guess he came out on top.

I could not believe Lilly put me through all that bullshit just so she could get a little bit of fame and a ring. In the end, I was nothing more to her than a glorified pool boy—good enough to fuck when the rich husband wasn't around but not worth giving up all that money for. Shit, as good as I fucked Lilly, she could have at least left me a few dollars on the nightstand.

Fuck the bitch! I loved her. I gave her my heart and soul, and she stomped on them like they were roaches under her pumps. I just don't get how she could be all over me one minute, all lovey-dovey, and then the next turn so cold. I would have given everything to her. Everything. My life even.

Lilly came up the winner. She got to fuck around and secure the money and a promotion too. What did I get? Just more loneliness.

After I left The Plaza that day, I called Lilly a few times. At first I just wanted to hear her say that I did not *really* witness her accepting Sig's proposal—that it was all my imagination. But when she didn't answer or return any of my calls or texts, I realized that what had transpired was not a hallucination. Lilly was going to be Sig's wife.

As I noted, I made only one more phone call after that epiphany. It was the last message I would ever leave for her. Of course, Lilly did not respond to that one either.

That voice message was supposed to be a purge for me. But it had no cathartic value whatsoever. It just left the whole mess open-ended and me a wreck. My mind seemed determined to obsess about Lilly. The first few thoughts of her always made me smile. I remembered her funny laugh, that Valley Girl voice, and how sweet she was to help me resolve the pain surrounding my mother. I actually missed her. However, the fact that she had blown me off and that haunting image of her accepting Sig's proposal reminded me that she was nothing to be upset over. She was just another user.

I sat in my living room with the shades drawn. My anguished headspace wanted nothing more than to disappear into the darkness. My only friends were the bottles of Jack Daniels now littering my home. I was not a heavy drinker by nature, but that whiskey got me through manic bouts of missing Lilly and despising her at the same time.

As occurs with all stupors, I was compelled to do something stupid, namely drunk dial Lilly. That's why I purposefully kept the phone on the other side of the room. However, I could not take my eyes off of it. It was a snake charmer, and I was a cobra. The more the phone enticed me to call, the longer my swigs became. That bottle was emptying fast, and I knew that my resolve not to call her would be nil when I ingested the last drop of booze.

A diversion was necessary. I did pick up that phone and dialed. I did not want to, but it was an emergency. A familiar voice answered.

"Hello?"

I wished like hell it was Lilly, but Rebecca had to do.

"Hey. What's up?" I said.

She paused, not pleased that I had neglected to call her for quite some time. "Nothing. Long time, no hear."

"Yeah, just busy," I said as I took another gulp of whiskey.

"I called you a few times…"

A few times? Woman, it was more like a million.

"When you didn't get back to me, I thought maybe you were mad or something else…like you had another girlfriend."

I knew she was probing me in her not-so-subtle manner. There was no way was I going to mention Lilly. I preferred to keep her to myself.

"Just busy. I called to see if you had any plans tonight. Do you want to come over?" I asked halfheartedly.

Rebecca inhaled with excitement like a child opening up a yearned-for Christmas gift. She must have caught the fireworks in her voice and took it down a notch. She was still peeved at my inattentiveness and was not going to reward me for it. "Why should I come over? I haven't heard from you in ages. What do you think I am? Some kind of booty call?"

Uh, yeah.

"No, of course not. I just really want to see you. Don't you want to see me too?"

"Yes," she said almost before I finished my sentence. "You don't mind that it's not Sunday night?"

I knew that this was yet another test question. She was really asking if I considered her my girlfriend. Normally, I would not have Rebecca over at any other time. But since Lilly was betrothed to another man, I figured, *What the fuck? Why not invite Rebecca over randomly?*

"I know what day it is, and I'm asking you to come over." I was not even thinking about the words coming out of my mouth. I was a robot speaking programmed words and phrases. I didn't give a shit.

"Okay, I'll be right over. Cam, I love—"

I hung up before she could finish. I didn't give a flying fuck how she felt about me. She had but one purpose—to make me forget about Lilly.

⁓

I stared down at the twenty-carat monstrosity on my left hand. I swear I needed a crane to lift my fucking finger.

The engagement ring was incredible. It somehow managed to trap all the rays of the sun and radiate them back out with an obnoxious brilliance that blinded anyone who dared to stare directly into it. That ring made it clear to everyone within a fifty-mile radius that I was Sig's property. I'm sure there was a chip hidden in the diamond, some sort of pussy-tracking device set upon a platinum band. Otherwise, I did not see the point in having an engagement ring of such ridiculous proportions.

I looked down at my ball and chain and wondered how Cam was doing. He had looked so hurt at The Plaza. It caused me pain just thinking about it. I had been trying to ignore my inner longing to see him again. I tried meditation, exercise, eating, sleeping, and even some degrading coitus with Sig. Yeah, sex with Sig. I figured the gross-out factor would be enough to make me not want sex with anybody else. Still, my mind, soul, and body continued to pulsate for Cam.

Though the reasons seemed right, being apart from Cam was sheer torture. My broken heart skipped beats as an eternity of hours slipped away. I had no more tears; I was cried out. Part of me knew I was supposed to be with Cam, that he was the one. The other part was well aware of the danger he faced if I tried to make that a reality.

Still, I believed that he was owed an explanation. No one should have their heart torn apart and not be given closure. That wasn't fair, and I knew it. I decided to take a chance and call Cam just to say I was sorry. Knowing him, I could not tell the truth. He would rail against not only Sig but Chief Pepperdine and Xander, which would surely lead to his death. I would give Cam some lame excuse that it was best this way— for me to marry Sig—and never see him again. I hoped that would not make him hate me too much. But if I were Cam, I would loathe me too.

I went to get my phone straightaway before I lost my nerve, but it was not in my purse. I hadn't seen it since The Plaza. I had no reason to use it. Tamara hated talking on the phone, and aside from her I had no real friends or family to contact. As far as business was concerned, I spoke to Sig directly.

I searched the house, every cranny of it, and panicked when I realized my phone wasn't there. I had not memorized Cam's number but had it on my cell. Now what was I going to do? Even if I could get his number again, I couldn't call from the house line. Sig would have a paper trail of my call. Besides, he probably had the phone tapped.

I sank to the marble floor, feeling defeated and totally alone. Then it dawned on me that Sig was caught up in his new business ventures and had not put much interest in keeping me in my cage. He figured I was trained enough that he could let go of my leash every once in a while. I made up my mind to go to Cam's home and tell him myself. I knew that was dangerous because something I did not want to experience would probably happen. Either Cam would curse me out, and I would feel like shit for the rest of my life, or we would end up in bed together, risking his life. Regardless, I still needed to have that final talk with him.

After much internal debate, I got in my car, trying not to think about the consequences if I got caught. I focused only on getting to Cam.

—————

My fist hovered in front of the door. I was terrified of knocking. I had no idea what to expect once Cam caught sight of me. I pulled my hand back and stalled a little by running my fingers through my hair and wiping down my coat.

Then I braced myself and knocked. I could hear some rumbling inside, but no one came out. I knocked again, harder this time. I could hear footsteps but found it strange that the steps were light, dainty even. What the fuck? I got a weird feeling that this whole scene was going to be bad. If I were in my right mind, I would have left right then and there. But when have I ever been in my right mind? I stayed put. Still, no one answered. I was just about to leave when the door finally creaked open.

A small woman was standing there. She was pretty—gorgeous, even. I stepped back and looked at the door and the surroundings to make sure I was in the right place.

"I'm sorry it took me so long, but I had to find some clothes to put on." She was wearing Cam's favorite college T-shirt from his alma mater and his sweatpants, which swamped her.

"Uh, I was looking for Cam," I said, totally bewildered. "Is he anywhere around? I'm sorry…who are you?"

The cute girl stretched out her hand. "I'm Becky."

I shook her hand and kept shaking it. This was the girl who left all those crazy messages on Cam's phone when we were in the mountains. My face started to contort as my eyes honed in on her. She was trying to take her hand back, but I was not letting go.

"Where's Cam? Is he in there?"

Becky was no dummy. Right then her intuition told her that I was not just some chick coming by for a casual visit. She knew that I was the reason for Cam's brief disappearance from her life. Becky yanked her hand out of mine.

"Cam's not here right now. He went out to get us breakfast. We had a long night, you know. Built up quite the appetite." She smirked. "You know how that is. You do have a boyfriend, don't you?"

Fucking cunt.

Becky was pushing it. She kept playing with the sweatshirt, trying to draw my attention to it. She saw me staring and made sure to rub it in.

"Oh, this old thing. This is my boyfriend's college sweat-shirt. Look at it…so many holes. I have told him a gazillion times to throw it away, but he just loves it. I guess it's my girl-friend duty to wear it. God, that man loves my scent on his clothes."

"His girlfriend? I was unaware that Cam had a girlfriend. He did mention that he was fucking some crazy bitch stalker, but never did he mention the word 'girlfriend' to me."

Becky knew I was talking about her and took a defensive posture. "Yeah, it's pretty clear that he has a girlfriend—me. We've been dating for over a year."

With that, she opened the door so I could see in. The room

was a tribute to a long night of fucking. Clothes were strewn all over the floor and furniture. Becky's nasty little thong was draped over a floor lamp, while Cam's boxers somehow managed to find a spot on the top shelf of his bookcase. From the way Cam's favorite chair had been moved haphazardly to the middle of the floor, I could tell it was caused by hardcore sex.

But the part that really singed me was the two plates on the dining table. That let me know that Cam had cooked for her. He told me he only cooked for someone special, and I thought that special one was me. How deluded was I?

Becky slyly closed the door enough to block the view of the room. She knew she had fucked with my head and started to chuckle. "You never told me who you were and why you wanted to see Cam."

I was two seconds away from grabbing the bun high on her head and slinging her scrawny ass to the floor. I wanted to scratch her fucking eyes out, kick her in her skanky twat, and take that sweatshirt for myself. My hand was rising to bitch slap her, but I caught myself. Becky was right. Cam was not my man. If she had a relationship with him for over a year and was there wearing his clothes, well, that made her his girlfriend in my opinion. I pocketed my hands. Becky had given me the closure I needed.

"Who am I? Just an old friend. I came to tell Cam good-bye," I finally answered as I turned around to leave.

"You going somewhere? Like a vacation?"

"No. It's just a good-bye." There was no need to turn back around. I just kept on walking away.

I heard Becky snicker as she closed the door. If that had happened a few minutes earlier, I would have been all over her. But now I had resolved that Cam and I were through. The elevator doors opened, and I stepped in and stood at the back. As the doors closed, I thought how that would be the last time I would ever see that place. I felt like shattered glass and looked down to see if any shards had fallen off me.

Driving through Midtown Manhattan was treacherous. The mayhem was not caused by insane cab drivers, dumbfounded tourists, or careless pedestrians. It was me. My mind was still reeling from my encounter with Becky, and its concentration level was at zero.

I pulled over and parked. Leaning my head against the steering wheel was the only thing that remotely calmed my nerves. That relief was infinitesimal. I needed to vent. But to who? I decided on Tamara—Old Faithful. There was a cell phone store across the street, and I went in to purchase two. I made sure I got my same account with my old number on one phone. The other one I designated as my throwaway phone that Sig would never find out about. I activated the old account in the store.

The phone displayed numerous calls and texts. Though I had not memorized Cam's number, I did recognize it. There was no need to listen the messages. So, one by one, I deleted them. Those messages were my last connections to Cam, and with them gone, it made it clear that he was gone too.

I pulled out my old-fashioned address book. It was really a simple mini spiral notebook that I kept random scrawls in. It was a garbled mess of shopping lists and ideas, but buried in the middle was Tamara's number, which I had also failed to memorize. I took a spot in the corner of the store by the window. I figured the miniscule amount of sunlight peeking through the dank sky would be enough of an antidote to my dreariness.

As the phone rang, I forced a smile to appear on my face. I didn't want Tamara to hear the sadness in my voice.

"Hello," she answered with her usual bubbly demeanor. Thank goodness because I needed it.

"It's me—Lilly." Whatever cheer I had was quickly leaving me.

"I hear a somber timber in your voice."

"I'm having a terrible day."

"What? Something happen between you and your fuck buddy? That dude with the chocolate eyes," Tamara joked.

"His name is Cam, and he wasn't a fuck buddy. Not that it matters. We're done anyway. That's why I'm calling you. I need a pep talk."

Tamara's voice thickened with severity. I could tell she wanted to give me an "I told you so." However, she opted to be a considerate friend instead.

"So you want to talk? That's what I'm here for." Her voice was so soothing, motherly. It made me feel like cradling in the nook behind me.

"It turns out Cam has a girlfriend. I went to his place, and she answered the door wearing his clothes," I confessed.

"Ouch."

"Yeah. He told me that she was nothing, just a fling. But she confirmed that they had been dating for at least a year."

A hand-holding couple passed by. They made me want to

puke. Why did they get to be so happy while I had to remain cursed when it came to love?

Tamara interjected some reason into my pity party. "The way I see it is that you really didn't lose anything. You knew Cam for all of a minute, and, from what I can tell, you two spent the bulk of your time in bed."

"It wasn't all about sex. We cared for one another. At least I did," I snapped.

"Look, I'm not saying that Sig is the best boyfriend in the world. But out of the two guys, he was the only one who made a commitment. I don't condone marrying for money, but you have been with Sig for a mighty long time. He was the more viable option."

Tamara only said that because I never let her know what Sig was really about. She just saw him as an emotionless asshole. To her, that might have been irritating but harmless. I never told her about the slaps, bites, threats, or Xander. I was always trying to save face and not look like a total idiot for putting up with his bullshit.

"And let's be real. You were sneaking around. You're the cheater. And you have the nerve to get made at Cam for doing the same thing to you," Tamara said with an ironic laugh. "So take off your nasty freak panties and put on your matrimonial ones. Those won't be as sexy, but they will be secure."

I burst into riotous laughter as the store's patrons wondered what the fuck was wrong with me. My mood was immediately elevated, and I felt like I could cope with the breakup. "Thanks, Tam. I don't know what I'd do without you."

"Yeah, I know. I am the best. But I've really got to go. Hugs and kisses."

"Hugs and kisses."

Tamara and I gave each other a "mwah" and hung up. I looked down at the phone. Even though I had deleted Cam's messages, I made sure to keep his number. I'm not exactly sure why. It wasn't like I'd need it or anything.

I was kidding myself again. My alter ego forced me to keep the number just in case I wanted to call Cam back. I would have spoken to him even if he had lingering traces of Becky on his breath. God only knows what they were doing.

Fuck. I am so pathetic.

Chapter Nineteen

My portion of Sig's case had wrapped up. On the surface, his financials appeared to be scrupulous. That was because of me. When it came to hiding assets or making strange expenses seem legitimate, I was a god. However, Wotherspoon and Associates still did not let me know who Z was. All I knew was that Z settled and was not going forward with a public lawsuit.

Whooptee-fucking-do.

I didn't care anyway. I was just glad that I didn't have to see Sig or Lilly ever again. Hell, even that fucking partnership no longer had any appeal. I don't know when I lost my passion for it. Probably when I lost Lilly.

It had been a few weeks since I had last seen her. Some days it felt like none of it had ever happened. Just a beautiful blur in my life. However, sometimes I wondered how she was doing. I would occasionally pass the meeting room when Sig came by, eavesdropping and hoping to find out what was happening in Lilly's world.

One time at the grocery store, I saw a local bridal magazine featuring an interview with her. I was flabbergasted by the speed in which the details of their engagement were already in print. Needless to say I didn't buy the magazine. I bought some more Jack Daniels and fucked Becky instead. Jack helped me bury my feelings for Lilly. Becky helped me bury my dick.

If I had been paying more attention and not waddling in self-pity, I would have noticed that I was being gunned for. Sig had seen me looking dejected despite my strong efforts to look *GQ*. I was certain he knew about Lilly and me. Therefore, I surmised he knew that my lackluster mood was caused by her absence.

Behind my back Sig had rallied not only Xander and Chief Pepperdine but Jacob. He told them that he knew about men like me. Men like me did not give up when it came to love. Sig was certain that I would come after Lilly, especially now that I had completed my part of the case. He had placed a briefcase on the table in front of those men. It was filled with neatly bound stacks of money, which he offered in exchange for participating in my murder.

Greed got the best of Chief Pepperdine and Jacob, and they eagerly agreed to the terms. Xander did not care much about the money. He was in it just for the joy of killing me.

Chapter Twenty

*C*am, *just fucking forget about Lilly. What is so fucking hard about that?*

I had taken a leave of absence from Wotherspoon and Associates just so I could mope in a pitch-black room. Though it was past midnight, I had no need to turn on any lights. The silent darkness gave me just enough solace to prevent me from losing my fucking mind completely. Any amount of luminance would have shed light on the derelict condition I was in. There was no way I could face that. The best I could do was to stand at the window and swig down the rest of the Macallen whiskey—a change from my regular Jack. After my last gulp, I held the bottle upside down, hoping to discover one more drop. As I tapped the bottle, I noticed a strange black car creeping past my building.

A car driving on a New York street normally would not have seemed odd. However, this vehicle made the hairs on the back of my neck stand as stiff as surgical needles. Whoever was driving could not see me as the darkness concealed my silhouette. They felt safe in maintaining a snail's pace that any elderly woman could outrun.

I kept my eye on the car until it rounded the corner, and the red haze of its brake lights faded away. A weird twinge cramped my belly as I turned from the window. I guess that's why I had to go back and do a double take. Indeed, the car was gone from my line of sight. Still, that ominous feeling remained. I headed toward my bed, not even realizing that I had picked up my trusty Louisville slugger.

That lapse in thought had become common with me since my apparent breakup—or whatever the fuck you call it—with Lilly. I was numb, disconnected not only from my mind but my body. I dropped down onto the dirty sex sheets that I had been fucking Becky on. I didn't care about the hygiene; I didn't care about anything anymore.

I had lost all shame with Becky and treated her worse than diarrhea coming out of a donkey's ass. To rid myself of my own pain, I gave it to her instead in the form of some pretty fucked-up sex. I did all manner of foul shit to her; I degraded her in every way I could think of. I must have been on the verge of going totally psycho because that was the only semblance of being alive I had left.

That's what Lilly did to me. That bitch.

Once again I tilted the empty bottle of whiskey right over my mouth. There was nothing left, but that didn't stop me from licking the opening for any remnants. When none were found, I threw the bottle against the wall, leaving a nice hole for me to fix later. Instead of jonesing for liquor I was not going to get, I settled for the white noise of mindless television.

I had no real interest in watching the cheesy '70s action movie. The purpose of the disjointed racket was really to give me the illusion that I wasn't alone. Exhausted from grief, I lay on my back while my bleary eyes stared at the ceiling. I imagined Lilly's spectral image hovering above me, smiling seductively and teasing me to take her. I reached out and grasped nothing but air—a stark reminder of the empty relationship we'd shared.

If I were a praying man, I would have begged God to intervene and take away the pain-filled crevasse that was my heart. I opted to close my eyes instead and let sleep give me a brief respite from the crushing torment.

Later that night a startling, sharp noise woke me. I propped up on my elbows and looked at the TV. A bottle blonde was shooting the equivalent of a pop gun at some ridiculous caricature of a criminal mastermind. With the massive number of wings in her hair, the actress could have just flown away. The thought of it made me laugh for the first time in weeks, and I turned down the volume.

Then I heard another noise like something falling outside my front door. I picked up my bat and cautiously made my way toward the ruckus. I opened the door slowly. The hallway was slightly illuminated by a small window at the other end. I was determined to inspect my property and stepped into the hall. As I made my way to the elevator, I kept turning in a circle in an attempt to protect myself from all sides.

I heard the ding of the elevator. The car was coming up, which meant someone was in my building. I took up post on the side of the elevator and waited for the dumb-ass intruder to come out. The number above the elevator went from one to two, and then the doors opened. I bum rushed the car, swinging with all my might. But the elevator was empty. Because I was not paranoid by nature, I assumed that there had been a mechanical glitch and decided to have it checked out the next day.

Confident, I strode back to my apartment and locked the

door. It took my mind a few seconds to register what happened next. When it did, I realized that I was being choked to death from behind. I tried to hold on to my bat, but my desire to fight for breath won out, and I dropped it. My hands furiously grabbed at my assailant, to no avail. Whoever it was, he was a towering mass of dense muscle. He stood steady behind me, rigid and strong, as if my tussling did not faze him at all.

I was rapidly losing consciousness, but somehow Lilly popped into my head. For some reason this gave me the resolve to continue battling for my life. I elbowed the asshole in his ribs, mentally disarming him just long enough for me to slip out of his grip. I swung around and pushed him back into the darkness. All I could see was a giant shadow facing me. His heaving breath was filling the room with heat.

"What? Scared to show your face, motherfucker?" I asked with indignation.

Xander emerged from the blackness. I was not surprised to see him. I knew that he would be coming for me one day. He was enjoying the fulfillment of my execution and wanted to savor every moment of it. He watched me for a bit like someone looking at a juicy steak behind the butcher counter. His fissured tongue licked his lips as a gleefully fiendish smile appeared. I could not believe this sick fucker was actually getting off on killing me.

But I was not an easy piece of game. I was a predator too. And it was obvious that between the two of us, someone was going to die. Xander had a physical advantage over me. I had to use whatever tools I had available. He was all brawn and no brain; I would start there.

"I know why you're here. It's because of Sig. He knows

about Lilly and me. Despite that motherfucking engagement, I could come get her if I wanted her. That drives him crazy. That's where you come in," I said to Xander, who was watching me, apparently hypnotized by my words. "Sig couldn't do his own dirty work. So he sent a stupid, dumb, mute sucker like you to do it for him. Tell me, what's it like to be Sig's stank pussy boy?"

That did it. No man, no matter how stunted, wants to be called a stinky cunt.

Xander's grin dissolved from his face, and he was on me in one second flat. He threw me to the ground. That asshole pushed my temples together like my head was a grape as he beat it against the floor. I could almost hear my skull cracking. I pounded the shit out of him the best I could. Even though I had been an athlete and worked out regularly, Xander was a crazed behemoth of rage. He was much bigger than me, and I found it nearly impossible to fight him off.

When Xander saw that I was about to pass out, he pulled his gun from his waistband. He opened and spun the cylinder. There were three bullets randomly placed in the chamber. Xander popped the cylinder back and put the muzzle to my forehead. I closed my eyes right before he squeezed the trigger. Apparently, that chamber was empty. Xander looked disappointed and promptly squeezed the trigger again. The next cylinder was empty also. I got no relief from that, realizing my luck was running out. But before Xander squeezed again, I somehow managed to swiftly push the gun toward the bed as he was taking his shot. The bullet hit the down pillow and caused a shower of feathers to rain above the bed. Xander positioned the gun to my head again. I knew I was a goner, but the funny thing about it was that I had no fear. I had lost Lilly, and nothing else seemed to matter to me.

That was until a heard a voice reminiscent of Lilly's. It told me that my life was not over yet and to do whatever it took to survive this. It instructed me to fuck with Xander's head one more time. The voice made no sense to me; I thought I was imagining it. But I was compelled to listen to it anyway. Besides, what did I have to lose except my life? In a supine position, there was no way I could get that beast off me. So I went about fucking with his remedial brain.

"You're not a real man? You can't fight with your own hands? You need a gun to make you feel tough? You had to come after me in the dark...a sneak attack. Figures. You were a punk then, and you're a fucking punk now. You wouldn't dare fight me mano a mano because you know that it would be nothing for me to beat your weak ass," I said, trying to goad Xander into a fist fight. It worked.

He put the gun down and let me stand up—more like wobble—on my feet. I blinked quickly to allow my blurred vision to return and saw him pushing up his sleeves. I was not about to give him the chance to jump me again and charged him immediately, making sure I got some kind of advantage. My surge sent Xander crashing into the wall. His burly body knocked down all my football and track trophies. He just laughed and stared at me with those vacant eyes then punched me dead in the face. Whiplash rocked my neck, and I fell backward. Xander came after me with full force, but I kicked him right in his balls when he got close enough. I hopped up and kneed him in the stomach. As he was doubled over, I pounded him on the back of his neck, and he dropped to the floor. I started toward my bat, but Xander reached out, grabbed my ankle, and tripped me. He dragged me back over to him. I went ape shit and waylaid the hell out of him.

Suddenly Xander threw me off and jumped up like gravity did not exist. I got up nearly as fast. We ran toward each other for the final conflict and dragged each other through that apartment like a tornado. Eventually Xander got the upper hand and subdued me from behind. He opened my mouth with both his hands and tried to rip my face apart. I could feel my jaw unhinging as he pulled my upper and lower teeth in two directions simultaneously.

Then I did what I never thought I would ever do in my life to another man. I grabbed Xander's dick and balls. As my fingers pulled downward, I dug them into Xander's flesh. I was trying to rip off his junk. I knew I had almost succeeded when I felt my fingertips touching from both sides of his dick like it was Silly Putty and the slipperiness of his blood spurting out. One more squeeze and his shit would have fallen to the floor. However, the gruesomeness of it all stopped me from completing the task. Xander looked at me then down at his bloody pants like he was in shock. I didn't hesitate and grabbed my bat. I split his concrete head open, causing blood to gush out like a spigot.

Like a human battering ram, I ran Xander all the way across the room, using the velocity to send him crashing out the window. He landed on the roof of that mysterious car, causing it to buckle deep into the passenger side of the interior.

The driver jumped out; it was Chief Pepperdine. He looked up at me then called for his lookout. A young man raced across the street. I recognized that boy from the gala. Jacob. Both men pulled an unconscious Xander from the roof and threw him into the car. Before Pepperdine got in, he gave me a sinister look. I knew they would be back, and there would be no mistakes next time. The assailants peeled out and drove away.

My first instinct was to call the cops. But, shit, how could I know who to trust? Any cop that came over could be an assassin. One thing was sure: I had to get out of my apartment.

As I threw random clothes into a suitcase, I played the surveillance footage from my security camera. I rewound too far back and saw an image of Lilly knocking on my door. I didn't remember seeing her on that particular day and watched more closely. As the video played, I saw Becky answer the door.

Aw, fuck! Lilly was here, and Becky didn't tell me.

As I watched Lilly walk to the elevator, I wondered how she could look so sad and radiantly beautiful at the same time. More important was that I realized she had not gotten over me. She wanted to reconcile but was intercepted by Becky. I had to get to her not only because she looked like she was not giving up on us. But because I had survived, she was probably in danger now.

I had gotten to know Sig's MO over the past few months. If he was going to hurt Lilly, it would not be tonight; he would be more careful than that. So I decided to lie low for a few hours. I would scope out Sig's house and monitor whether or not my attackers showed up. When everything was clear, I was going to get my woman.

Ever since I caught Becky at Cam's house, I had made considerable progress moving on from him. I had accomplished this mainly by occupying my time with the arduous details of planning an exclusive wedding. The endless lists of caterers, florists, and musicians almost made me forget Cam even existed.

Though Sig was not the man I had envisioned my future with, I was resolved to my fate and decided to make the best of it. I mean what was so terrible about it? I had my dream job, a mansion here in the States as well as homes all over the world, and more money than I could spend in a lifetime. I chalked Cam up to experience and started a new chapter in my life.

As I perused yet another bridal magazine, I heard the chime of the intercom notifying me that someone was at the front gate. *Who the hell is that?* I asked myself as I walked over to answer. "Hello?"

All I heard was the breath of a man.

Really.

Occasionally some of Sig's groupies would show up and do silly shit like that. "Please go away before I call the police," I said indifferently.

Then an urgent voice spoke up. "Lilly, don't hang up. It's Cam."

I shook my head, in no way believing it was really him. I backed away while the intercom buzzed incessantly. After centering myself, I pressed the button again. "Cam, is that really you?"

"Yes, Lilly. It's me. I have to talk to you."

Full-body flutters filled me up as a wide smile enveloped my face. But as I was about to open the gate, I remembered something. Cam had been fucking Becky for a year and conveniently left out that detail. He was a piece of shit. This thing with Becky...well, I could not get past it.

"Did you bring your little girlfriend with you?"

"What? What are you talking about? You mean Becky? That's what I'm here to explain along with something much more important."

"Fuck you, Cam. I trusted you, and you fucked around behind my back. You let me down."

There was a momentary silence, and then he let me have it. "Me! I let you down? You made me believe that we had a real connection, that you actually gave a good goddamn about me. The minute I turned my back on you, you got engaged to your puppeteer. All I did was love you. All you did was shit on me."

Cam had some fucking nerve jumping on me. I disconnected from the intercom, giving him a metaphorical good riddance. The next thing I knew, I heard an incredibly loud crash. Cam, that fool, had rammed the front gate. I went to the phone to call 911 but thought, *Fuck that*. I would confront him myself.

I opened the front door and stormed outside to meet him. I heard the familiar rumble of his motorcycle rapidly approaching. Though I was pissed off, there was still no sweeter sound. My heart was beating out of my chest with tartness and anticipation.

Like an angry archangel materializing, Cam appeared out of the morning fog. He made an abrupt stop, sliding his bike right in front of me.

"You've got some damn nerve being here! And my gate? You know you're going to pay for that, right?" I said, pointing my finger in his face.

"Fuck your goddamn gate. I came to tell you that I saw you with Becky on surveillance. After you got engaged, I needed something, anything to take my mind off you. Since you came by my apartment, I figured you may still feel something for me. That's why I'm here. But fuck trying to make nice with you. I'm also here to warn you. Sig tried to have me killed last night. That means you may be fucked too."

All of my bravado disappeared. "Sig told me that he wouldn't bother you if I married him."

"You're only marrying him to protect me?" Cam asked, calming down.

"Yes. Why the hell else do you think I would do some stupid shit like that?"

Since Sig reneged on his promise not to kill Cam, all bets were off. Besides, it had been too long since Cam and I had seen or touched each other. We stood frozen, stunned by one another's presence. Then, like magnets, we ran into a desperate embrace. Lightning pulsed through me, torching my soul. All my despair was cremated by Cam's touch. I nearly forgot how good he smelled and took deep pulls of his heady scent. It did not bother me that he smelled like an atomic mixture of sweet sweat and alcohol.

I pulled back to take a closer look at him. That's when I noticed that Cam's nose was smeared with dried blood and his eye was blackened. "What happened?" I asked as I stroked his face.

"Xander," Cam replied.

"I know what kind of cretin he is. He got me too."

"He hurt you? Why didn't you tell me? If I had known that, I would have made sure to kill him last night. I will destroy anything or anyone who hurts you. I love you that much."

"I love you too."

Then it happened. The kiss. The kiss that I had been denied for weeks. An inner quake broke the parched earth inside of me. I was so overwhelmed that I went totally limp in Cam's muscular arms. Lightheadedness resulted from the blood rushing from my brain to my pussy. It welled up, a juicy fount of love that waited for Cam to take a drink. Reuniting not only got me going. It aroused Cam also. I could feel that luscious dick swelling against me. I ran my hand along its long shaft and took the head, which I worked like a snake. I could see the steam of Cam's deep breaths leaving his nostrils as he gripped my ass.

All of a sudden he grabbed my hands. "As much as I want to take you, we don't have time for that. We are now in the fight for our lives. I promise that I'm not going to lose you again. The only way we can be together is to get Sig out of the way. We've got to do that right now. There's no more time to waste."

"How the hell are we going to do that? Sig has bought and paid for cops all over this city and then some. We can't trust anybody. And let's not even get into Xander."

I could see Cam thinking. I knew he came up with an answer when a mischievous smile crossed his face. "I've been working on Sig's financials. There is some fucked-up shit in there that you have no clue about. Do you know anyone with the initial Z?"

"No."

"Well, Sig has some shady arrangements concerning this Z. There's a secret file in Wotherspoon's office. I have a feeling it has some incriminating evidence that we could use against Sig. That way, he would leave us alone. The problem is that security at Wotherspoon and Associates is about as tight as Fort Knox. Those guards actually have orders to shoot to kill."

"So what are you going to do? Are you going to get those files?"

"It's the only way."

"Cam, I don't know about that. I already lost you once. I don't want to lose you permanently."

"Don't worry. I promise I'll be back. What I need you to do is hang tight. If Sig calls, pretend that everything is copasetic. Don't make him suspicious in any way."

I had the sinking feeling that I was looking at a dead man. I had to hug Cam so I could take my pained eyes off of him. "Please be careful and come back to me."

He gave me one last kiss before he got on his bike and rode away. I turned around and saw Lin standing at the door. Apparently, she had seen the whole thing. I thought she would judge me. However, she gave me a supportive nod like she agreed with the actions I was taking. She went back to sweeping the floor as if nothing had happened and she was there merely doing her job.

Lin respectfully opened the door for me when I walked back in. I gave her a hug. I know it was off-putting to her, but that was my way of saying thanks. She hesitated and then returned the favor.

Chapter Twenty-One

I braved going back to my apartment so that I could get a quick shower and shave and put on one of my finest suits. If I was going to infiltrate Mr. Wotherspoon's office, I had to at least look like I belonged on the twenty-sixth floor.

My apartment was a mess. Not only from the fight but because someone had come back and ransacked it, looking for Xander's gun. They were not going to find it. It was in my possession now.

I rifled through some of the shit that was strewn all over the floor. I picked up my childhood photo album and my mother's old cookbook and headed to the door. I looked back one more time at my home. It would no longer be the same; it was violated and contaminated with too many terrible memories now. After today, I could never come back to it.

Good-bye, buddy.

I closed the door on my old life and headed to Wotherspoon and Associates. With my knapsack on my back filled with my few precious possessions, I breezed through traffic, getting my game plan together. It was simple enough: do whatever it took to get that file.

By the time I arrived at Wotherspoon and Associates, I felt surprisingly calm. They had not disabled my iris recognition, so I was able to walk through the lobby undetected. I took the elevator up to my office as if nothing was amiss. However, that was not the case for everyone else there. When I stepped out onto the fifth floor, I noticed a thick tension in the air, and everyone was looking at me. Robert rushed over.

"Dude, not a good day to be here," he said, looking around all jittery.

"Why? What's going on?"

"Wotherspoon, that Krok asshole, and their monkey, Xander, were all in a tizzy this morning. They were questioning everyone about your whereabouts. They left, but before they did, they went into your office. What's up with that?"

"Beats me. I'll go up to the twenty-sixth floor to see what's going on."

"And your fucking eye? What happened? Xander had a bandage on his head too. What, you two had a fight?" Robert joked.

"Yeah, right."

Robert was still talking and laughing at his own joke when I started walking away. He even made reference to Xander's painful gait, like he had been fiercely kicked in the balls. That tidbit of information put a devilish smirk on my face. But it also made it clear that Xander was nearly unstoppable.

When Robert finally realized that I was no longer listening to him and was halfway across the room, he went back to his desk to catch up on busy work. I went into my office and got my name plate. Though I knew I would not work for the firm any longer, I was determined to get it. I earned that motherfucker.

I proceeded to the twenty-sixth floor, where I saw Linda stationed in front of Mr. Wotherspoon's office. Shit, that fucking cloven-hooved bitch was the only thing standing between me and that file. I tried to disappear into the wallpaper without her noticing me. I caught a break when one of the associates asked her to accompany him to the copy room.

That was my chance. I ghosted my way into Wotherspoon's office and shut the door. Thankfully, the blinds were already closed. I wasted no time going to the wall safe. I remembered back to when I saw Mr. Wotherspoon open it with the numbers of his birth date. However, I still did not have the last digit… the wildcard.

I could hear the old hag's voice in the distance as she was coming back. I had to hurry. I failed to open the safe with every combination, one through eight. With each twist of the dial, I could hear Linda's voice growing closer. If she caught me, she would immediately call security, and there would be no telling how they would dispose of me. I finally cracked the combination with the number nine. I grabbed all the files I could fit into my hands. Then I slipped out of the office just in the nick of time, with Linda barely missing me.

I walked as fast as I could without drawing suspicion and took the back stairs. My escape did not go off without a hitch, though. Jacob caught sight of me just as I exited the door. That little rectum immediately notified security. I was almost to the sixth floor when I heard the alarms blaring. I could hear all the doors leading from the central staircase to the rest of the floors starting to lock down. I dipped through one of them right before it locked and trapped me in the stairwell. I was on a floor that was being renovated.

Through clear plastic, I saw that a window cleaner had parked his suspended platform in front of the glassless opening. That was my way out. He nearly had a heart attack when I suddenly ripped the plastic off the window hole and poked my head out like a madman. I read his nametag—Johnnie.

"Johnnie, I could really use a ride down," I said, flashing a one-hundred-dollar bill.

That bologna-and-cheese sandwich he was holding no longer interested Johnnie as he snatched the money out of my hand. I climbed out the window, and he lowered me down. As we descended, I peeked into the windows on each floor. I could see an army of security guards frantically looking for me with guns drawn. They had orders to kill on sight.

"Could you hurry it along a bit?" I asked Johnnie.

He looked at me like he could not be bothered but quickened his pace anyway.

As I stepped off the platform on ground level, my stomach lashed out and growled at the world. I grabbed Johnnie's sandwich and took a bite.

"Sorry, man. It's been one of those days." I handed the sandwich back to Johnnie and sprinted off the platform, eager to make my way back to Lilly.

The head of security had made a phone call to Mr. Wotherspoon and informed him of the happenings. Sig was still with him and had a feeling that a search of the building was futile. He knew I was headed to the mansion to retrieve Lilly and had ordered his henchmen to greet us there.

I paced nervously, waiting for Cam to return. This was it—the day I was leaving all the money and glamour behind. I didn't bother to take down my prepacked suitcase. It was not so much because there would be no way to carry it on the back of Cam's bike. It had more to do with me saying "fuck you" to all the bullshit Sig had put me through. I was leaving anything connected to him behind. I was leaving with what I had come with, just the clothes on my back. And that was fine with me.

The house phone rang. I knew it could only be one person. I took a deep breath and answered, making sure I sounded like everything was just fine. "Hello, Sig."

I could detect tension on the other end of the line.

"What are you doing?" he asked. I could tell he was making sure I was not with Cam.

"Nothing. Just looking over bridal magazines. What's going on with you?"

Sig hung up in my face. He had no interest in how my day was going. He was only concerned that I was playing the obedient dupe and that Cam was not here with me.

More importantly, Sig's call meant that Cam had breached the inner lair of Mr. Wotherspoon's office, and they were now hunting him down. This also let me know that Cam was still alive because if they had killed him, Sig would not have had a reason to call.

Yes!

It didn't take long for Cam to finally show up with the mysterious files. I greeted him at the door with the most exuberant hug, jumping into his arms and nearly knocking him to the ground. Cam, in turn, gave me a boggling kiss that was about to send both of us to the bedroom. Even in this life-and-death situation, I wouldn't have minded a quick fuck. However, Cam came to his senses and pulled his lips from mine. He immediately returned to the task at hand.

"Lilly, as much as I would like to indulge in the wonderments of your body, we really don't have much time. They're after me…us. I barely got out of the office alive. I hope you're ready because we've got to get out of here now."

"Let's rock," I said as I grabbed my coat. As I sleeved my arms, I looked around at the house and could not help but shiver at the thought that I wasted so much of my life there. Cam could see me quake and comforted me by taking my hand.

Looking deep into my eyes, he said, "I know it's scary to give up the only thing you have known, even if it sucked your soul out of you. Change never comes easy. But a whole new life is waiting for you. A life that you'll share with me. So don't look back. Staying tethered to the past will do nothing but plunge a dagger through your heart. It's time to go."

As Cam led me across the front door's threshold, I had a realization. Sig was a slippery worm, and I knew that Cam and I would only have one shot to get this right. We needed all the evidence we could get to destroy Sig once and for all. I stopped Cam in his tracks.

"We can't leave yet," I said.

"What? There are murderers on their way here right now. They're not coming to negotiate or spend quality time with us. They're coming to kill us, and they will if we don't go."

"I know it sounds crazy. And it is dangerous. But there might be some more incriminating evidence on Sig's computer. He's on that thing all the time and acts suspicious when I come around it. I just have a feeling that there's something that can be used against him in court. At the very least I think he has another woman. Maybe that woman is Z. If so, Z may be able to help us."

Cam let out a sigh; he knew I was right. He looked around at the property, scoping it out for any hidden dangers. All was quiet…for now.

"It's worth a shot, but we've got to hurry," he said. "Where's the computer?"

I took Cam to Sig's private office and shut the door behind us.

"What did you do that for? We need to be able to see what's going on in the rest of the house at all times," he said as he kept watch at the window.

I closed doors behind me out of habit. Sig had terrorized me for the past few years. Whenever he was frustrated at the world, he would use me as a surrogate punching bag. I learned early on to lock the doors behind me after a particularly brutal set of sneak attacks. But there would be no more of that. Cam had emancipated me from Sig's slavery, and I opened the door without giving it another thought.

Cam waved a DVD imprinted with the letter Z in front of him. "I got this from Mr. Wotherspoon's office today along with the paperwork. Do you have a DVD player?" he asked with total sincerity.

I laughed. "Really? Sig is one of the wealthiest men in the universe, and you actually ask me if we have a DVD player. He could buy a million DVD players. But you only need one, and it's right behind you."

Cam and I both enjoyed that fleeting moment of levity. We didn't dwell on it and immediately went about our search for evidence against Sig. As Cam set up the DVD player, I tried to figure out the password to Sig's computer. I tried about twenty different combinations and started to accidentally repeat them.

Deciding to write the failed combinations on a piece of paper to keep track, I opened one of Sig's unused leather-bound notebooks and reached for a gold pen. Due to my nervousness, my clumsy hand knocked the pen to the floor. As I went to retrieve it, I discovered a series of passwords taped to the underside of Sig's desk. All of them were crossed out except the last one. I reasoned that it was his current password and typed it in. The computer sprang to life.

At the same time, Cam started the DVD. He stood back with his arms folded as he watched the first grainy images appear. I could see him squinting as he tried to figure out what was going on. It was becoming obvious that two people were having sex.

I watched, too, and cocked my head to the side as the image displayed sodomy. "So Z is some kind of porn star?" I asked.

Then the screen cleared up a bit more. I saw that one of the two people on the video was Sig. He was the top.

"That asshole was fucking around on me after all."

However, the horror I felt was intensified when the identity of the other person was revealed. Z, it turned out, was at most a fourteen-year-old Thai boy. My breathing stopped, and I felt my brain about to explode. I cramped with actual physical pain as I watched Sig violate this boy's body. Disgusted, Cam quickly turned off the DVD. He was as stupefied as I was.

"What the shit was that?" he asked as if he had just come back from a demonic alternate universe.

I looked back over at the computer. The screen was filled with everyday poses and sickening sexual images of Z. I investigated more and found hundreds of hours of chat logs between Sig and the boy. Apparently Sig was very much in love with him. If it were not so perverted and had been between two consenting adults, those same messages would have been incredibly romantic.

In light of my discovery, strange things regarding Sig and me started to make sense. I now understood why he wanted me to be so thin. It had nothing to do with modeling or his idea of a trophy girlfriend. Sig's obsession with my thinness had to do with his desire for me to look like a prepubescent boy. Also, the chat log and DVD explained why Sig only wanted to fuck me from behind. Sick bastard.

The irony of the situation did not escape me. My father, my tormentor, was also a pedophile. And here I was attaching myself to another one. Looking back, all the men I had been involved with had had a negative aspect of my father.

Boy, did I know how to pick them.

Sig just happened to be the composite of all that was shitty about my father. With him, I had tried to fix and reconcile my past, and had gotten nothing but more agony instead. However, I had broken part of the chain with Cam. I now had a man who was decent, kind, and a protector. Was I finally done with my past? That was the question I still had to answer.

"That explains it all," Cam said.

"Explains what?" I was trying not to vomit in response to what I had just seen.

"Why Sig didn't want to see Z harmed. Z was blackmailing Sig and wanted a tremendous amount of money to keep quiet about their relationship. Sig's normal way to deal with difficult people is to dispose of them. He could have had Z murdered at any time, especially in Thailand, but he chose not to. Instead, he wanted to support the boy and protect himself at the same time. That's why I was brought in to create a false financial paper trail just in case things didn't work out."

I rubbed my stomach, craving an antacid. "I think we have what we need, but we can't go to the cops. So where do we go?"

Cam already had the answer. "I know exactly who to take this shit to."

We gathered up the evidence and headed back to New York City. The back road taking us into town was clear of traffic. I felt somewhat relieved as I gripped Cam tightly around his waist. As the chilly wind whipped around us, I thought I was on the precipice of heaven. I would enter its gates as soon as we exposed Sig. However, the anticipation of a joyous future did not last long.

A grim, shadowy SUV with blacked-out windows was approaching us from the opposite direction. Cam did not seem concerned; he just throttled his bike. As we closed in on the SUV, it suddenly veered into our lane and was mere inches from hitting us head on. Cam swerved sharply off the road and barely missed a tree. I almost fell off the bike as it plowed through the rough terrain. Cam tried to put us back on the road due to the massive amounts of trees and brush in the forest. The motorcycle hit the asphalt violently. Cam almost lost control but quickly regained it. We took off at full speed down the hilly, curvy road. The SUV made a U-turn and promptly chased us down.

The passengers in the SUV pulled out Uzis and fired bursts of lead at us from both sides. One of these men was Xander. I ducked as I heard bullets whizzing past my head. Cam kept swerving in and out of lanes, making sure we would not be static targets.

The shooting wasn't killing Cam and me fast enough, so

the driver floored the vehicle. He caught up to us and tried to ram the back of the motorcycle. After some successful evading on Cam's part, the SUV eventually tapped the back of the bike slightly and almost caused us to lose control a few times. I looked over Cam's shoulder and saw that we were approaching the most dangerous curve on the road. If they hit us there, Cam and I would most certainly die.

There was also black ice ahead that none of us was aware of. The SUV attempted to ram the bike once more, but Cam shifted over just in time. Unknowingly, he had missed the black ice. However, the SUV did not.

It hit the black ice and slid hard as the driver overcorrected. The SUV flipped and rolled into a thick bank of trees. After buckling like a can of sardines, it caught on fire. Cam drove us to a safe enough distance and skidded to a stop. I looked back as the SUV exploded into a massive fire ball. I could see Xander writhing in agony as broken bones jutted out of his skin and the fire burned him alive. As he died, his eyes were fixated on me. I was glad that I was the last thing he saw before he went to hell. Even though it might have been morbid, that put a big smile on my face.

Cam did not want to waste more time contemplating the bonfire and got us to New York City at warp speed. As we made our way through traffic, I wondered who he was going to give the evidence to. We finally ended up at New York's most popular television network—but of course there was no parking on the crowded street. Cam was in such a rush that he hopped the bike on the sidewalk and drove through a legion of shocked pedestrians. We parked right in front of the doorman, and Cam threw him the keys.

"Handle that," he said to the incredulous doorman. The guy

got over his surprise, shrugged his shoulders, and proceeded to drive Cam's motorcycle to whatever parking garage he could find.

Cam and I ran through the network's lobby and happened to see the most famous and adored evening news anchor, Lucy Watts. We ran up to her like a couple of kooks.

"Ms. Watts, we've got something you have to see," Cam said.

I could tell that she was about to have security pounce all over us. However, she stopped when she recognized me. The opportunist in Ms. Watts took over, and she was all of a sudden eager to talk.

"I cannot believe Lilly Amsel is standing in front of me. Did you know I've been trying to get an interview with you for years? Don't take that the wrong way. I've always been a personal fan of your work, Ms. Amsel. Or should I say Mrs. Krok?"

My bullshit detector was singing. I knew that she was just like the rest of them, only interested in me because of Sig. But if Cam thought this lady could help us fuck Sig, I could tolerate her for at least a little while.

"Call me Ms. Amsel. I'll never be Mrs. Krok. After you see this, you'll understand why."

Ms. Watts took the DVD I held out. Her mouth salivated at the thought of an exclusive about Sig and me. She rushed us into her dressing room like a desperate car salesman protecting his claim over a potential buyer.

Striped pink and magenta, her frilly dressing room was more fit for a movie star than a newscaster. A white shag

carpet and gargantuan flower arrangements made it feel somewhat claustrophobic. I noticed that Cam was having a terribly
difficult time finding a comfortable place to sit on the couch,
which was smothered with large accent pillows. Ms. Watts had
specialty tea already brewing and took out dainty cups.

"Would you care for some tea? I got it when I was on assignment in Japan." She was trying to pull an Oprah, loosening us
up in an effort to make sure we spilled all of Sig's secrets.

"We really want you to see the DVD," I said. The more time
we chatted about Japanese tea, the more time Sig had to cover
his tracks.

"I was just being polite," Ms. Watts said as she examined
the DVD. "What is it? The story of the century?"

"Maybe," Cam responded.

"That's what they all say," she responded before casually
popping in the DVD.

At first Ms. Watts sweetly sipped her tea. However, Cam
and I both watched as her face started to twist.

"What is this? Is that Sig Krok and a young boy? It can't
be," she said as a tear trickled down her cheek. Ms. Watts was
not crying only because she witnessed a child being raped but
because her fantasy about Sig and me had been obliterated. I
felt so guilty about what I had just done to her. I forced her eyes
to see a horror that no one should be exposed to. She would
never be the same after that. But it had to be done.

"This goes on tonight," she announced as she wiped her
mascara-blurred eyes.

Cam and I holed up at a hotel in Midtown and sustained ourselves with a buffet of Chinese takeout. As chopsticks entered our hungry mouths, we watched the six o'clock news. The lead story was about Sig, presented by Lucy Watts.

It didn't take long for the entire world to react with utter revulsion. However, Cam and I celebrated as we tapped egg rolls like they were champagne goblets, knowing we had done a good job.

Not to mention that my pussy became Cam's fortune cookie later on that night. He cracked it open and ate it ferociously. His fortune read: *I am yours forever.*

Chapter Twenty-Two

I stood in front of the mirror in the new apartment I shared with Cam, looking at how I had changed during the past twelve months. There were no bruises to hide or broken bones to set. I noticed that my reflection was softer, not as hard and sharp as it had been when I lived with Sig.

There was a question I had asked myself long ago. Was I finally done with my past? The answer was yes. I was done with all that shit. I smiled, proud of the woman I now was. The memory of my father was an ancient blur. Some days it was like he'd never existed. Also, I no longer gave a fuck what other people thought about me. Shit, they had to worry about what I thought about them. As for the pills, I had no desire for them.

I thought back to a year ago today. Back then Sig was hiding in a closet at the mansion when national and Interpol police found him. I could not believe it. His dumb ass actually hid in a closet. How appropriate. Needless to say the Klå empire crumbled in light of its child-labor violations and Sig's pedophilia. Sig was now in prison and had to be sequestered in solitary confinement because of the endless beatings and ass raping he received on a daily basis.

The principals at Wotherspoon and Associates went to prison, too, along with Chief Pepperdine. It was absolutely hilarious to watch them rat each other out like little bitches. Hopefully, they were being ass fucked too.

Jacob had no one to back his modeling dreams and wound up back in Idaho. The last I heard, he was downgraded to doing the occasional fashion show at a local strip mall. However, he had to retire when he'd gained fifty pounds.

Cam eventually had to put a restraining order on Rebecca. She just could not accept the fact that he had dismissed her. But hardcore love never just goes away. That's why when Cam and I were out and about, I sometimes got the heebie jeebies. I sensed Rebecca was always close by. Cam believed it was all just my imagination, but I knew she was still prowling around in the dark.

I was tainted by Sig's sick escapades for a few months. It was difficult for the public to disassociate me from his image since that's what I had built my career and life on. The media scrutiny and notoriety made it impossible for me to procure modeling assignments. But that didn't matter to me so much. After all, I was only using modeling to ingratiate myself with powerful people and receive validation through my looks. Those same people that I pursued quickly turned their backs on me after the scandal—all except Tamara. In addition to Cam, she became a source of strength for me. I don't know what I would have done without her constant support.

My healing took place, and I was able to throw away my crutch called professional modeling. I now taught troubled girls etiquette, which I learned while living among the elite. I taught them a little modeling, too, but I also mentored them on developing self-esteem. I never wanted to see another young woman end up like I did.

Cam left the ruthless world of corporate law behind him and became a child-advocate lawyer instead. It made him feel good to rescue children who were placed in the sometimes brutal foster care system. Through his diligence, many children found healthy, loving homes. I was so proud to call him my man.

After that contemplation of the past year and my new life, I stepped away from the mirror with satisfaction. I went to the closet at the back of my bathroom and pulled out my black lingerie and stiletto heels. I slipped on my thigh-high stockings, admiring my smooth skin. I seductively put on the rest of the sheer lingerie. My inner goddess had killed my alter ego, allowing me to have complete control over my sexual destiny.

I put on my stilettos then went to a small red box I had stashed in the cabinet. I opened it and pulled out a pair of handcuffs, studying the links as I dangled them on my index finger. It was time to play. I gave myself one more look in the mirror then traipsed into the bedroom with the handcuffs hidden behind my back.

Cam was on the edge of the bed leaning back, waiting for me. He was cool and self-assured as usual, ready to take full control of the situation. He looked divine sitting on the bed, and that made a part of me want *him* to take me. But I was the boss.

I revealed the handcuffs to Cam, letting them swing at my side teasingly. He knew I had decided to be the dominant one for a change and was taken aback. He was not used to being submissive. I gave him a naughty grin, and Cam decided to play along.

"You going to arrest me?" he asked.

I made my way over to Cam and forcibly handcuffed him then pushed him back and pulled off his pants. His gigantic cock had already sprung to attention. My love box's automatic response would normally have been to sit on top of it. However, today I would not listen to anything that would make me lose command of the situation. I tantalized Cam's dick with my tongue, letting him know who was in charge. Then my hot, wet mouth went all the way down on that big cock, giving it bites as I went back up. I made it hurt.

Cam didn't know what to make of this. He was swamped with ultimate pleasure and pain. As he moaned, I stopped. I would make him beg for it.

"More, more," he said huskily. He wanted to touch me but was hindered by the handcuffs.

I ran my tongue over him, sending torturous spasms of desire throughout his body. I gave him just enough to drive him crazy but not enough to satisfy. I hungrily watched Cam as my pussy got wetter and wetter. It excited me to see him in a submissive position for once. I temptingly pulled my panties down, exposing my shaved snatch. As Cam licked his lips, I could see that first little bead of cum leak out of the tip of his rod.

I climbed on top and lowered my pussy down over his hard shaft, slowly moving up and down. Cam struggled to grip my breasts but was once again impeded by the handcuffs. I reached back and stroked his balls as I confidently fucked him, exhilarated by being the chief of this sexual encounter. I didn't need Cam to stimulate my nipples. With my free hand, I did that for myself. Between fucking Cam and my auto-erotica, I came hard. I was inundated by multiple orgasms and was still cumming when Cam shot his load into me.

After I rolled off, I continued clenching and spasming for a few minutes. Consumed with my own bliss, I forgot that Cam was still handcuffed. He lifted up his wrists.

"Hey, Sheriff, what about me?"

"Oh, yeah. You've been bailed out," I said as I retrieved the key from the bathroom. I released Cam, and he invited me to snuggle in his arms. I was proud of myself for taking charge. I would never have done that a year ago.

Would I go through all that hell again? That goes without saying. I would go through a thousand hells and more to have Cam by my side.

Follow Gina Whitney

On Twitter
@ginamwhitney

On Facebook
https://www.facebook.com/ginawhitneyauthor

On her blog
http://authorginawhitney.blogspot.com

Made in the USA
San Bernardino, CA
14 May 2014